YORK NOTES

AN INSPECTOR CALLS

J. B. PRIESTLEY

NOTES BY JOHN SCICLUNA

Longman
is an imprint of

PEARSON

 York Press

YORK PRESS
322 Old Brompton Road, London SW5 9JH

PEARSON EDUCATION LIMITED
Edinburgh Gate, Harlow,
Essex CM20 2JE, United Kingdom
Associated companies, branches and representatives throughout the world

First published 1997
New edition 2002
This new and fully revised edition 2010

20 19 18 17 16 15 14
IMP 10 9 8

ISBN 978–1–4082–4873–7

Illustrations by Philip Harris; and Neil Gower (p. 6 only)

Photograph of J. B. Priestley used by kind permission of Corbis Images

Phototypeset by Carnegie Book Production
Printed in China (GCC/08)

CONTENTS

PART FOUR
KEY CONTEXTS AND THEMES

PART FIVE
LANGUAGE AND STRUCTURE

PART SIX
GRADE BOOSTER

Study and revision advice

here are TWO main stages to your reading and work on *An Inspector Calls*. Firstly, he study of the play as you read it. Secondly, your preparation or revision for exam r Controlled Assessment. These top tips will help you with both.

READING AND STUDYING THE PLAY – DEVELOP INDEPENDENCE!

- Try to engage and respond **personally** to the characters, ideas and story – not just for your enjoyment, but also because it helps you develop your own **independent ideas** and **thoughts** about *An Inspector Calls*. This is something that examiners are very keen to see.

- **Talk** about the text with friends and family; ask questions in class; put forward your own viewpoint – and, if time, **read around** the text to find out about *An Inspector Calls*.

- Take time to **consider** and **reflect** about the **key elements** of the play; keep your own notes, mind-maps, diagrams, scribbled jottings about the characters and how you respond to them; follow the story as it progresses (what do you think might happen?); discuss the main themes and ideas (what do *you* think it is about? Power? Family conflict? Class?); pick out language that impresses you or makes an **impact**, and so on.

- Treat your studying **creatively**. When you write essays or give talks about the play make your responses creative. Think about using really clear ways of explaining yourself, use unusual quotations, well-chosen vocabulary, and try powerful, persuasive ways of beginning or ending what you say or write.

REVISION – DEVELOP ROUTINES AND PLANS!

- **Good revision** comes from **good planning**. Find out when your exam or controlled assessment is and then plan to look at key aspects of *An Inspector Calls* on different days or times during your revision period. You could use these Notes – see **How can these Notes help me?** – and add dates or times when you are going to cover a particular topic.

- Use **different ways** of **revising**. Sometimes talking about the text and what you know/don't know with a friend or member of the family can help; other times, filling a sheet of A4 with all your ideas in different colour pens about a character, for example the Inspector, can make ideas come alive; other times, making short lists of quotations to learn, or numbering events in the plot can assist you.

- **Practise plans** and **essays**. As you get nearer the 'day', start by looking at essay questions and writing short bulleted plans. Do several plans (you don't have to write the whole essay); then take those plans and add details to them (quotations, linked ideas). Finally, using the advice in **Part Six: Grade Booster**, write some practice essays and then check them out against the advice we have provided.

EXAMINER'S TIP

Prepare for the exam or assessment! Whatever you need to bring, make sure you have it with you – books, if you're allowed, pens, pencils – and that you turn up on time!

Introducing *An Inspector Calls*

SETTING

An Inspector Calls is set in the fictional industrial city of Brumley. The action takes place on one evening just before the First World War, in the home of a prosperous factory owner, and shows us the difference in life style between those who owned the factories, and who had money and power, and those who depended on them for work.

The Birlings' House

The Police Station

Milwards

MILWARDS

The Factory

Palace Variety Theatre

Hospital/Mortuary

CHARACTERS: WHO'S WHO

MR BIRLING

MRS BIRLING

THE INSPECTOR

EVA SMITH / DAISY RENTON

GERALD CROFT

ERIC BIRLING

SHEILA BIRLING

J. B. PRIESTLEY: AUTHOR AND CONTEXT

1906 The Labour Party is founded after the success of the Labour Representation Committee in the General Election

1914–18 First World War. Aged 20, J. B. Priestley joins 10th Duke of Wellington's Regiment, and serves on the front line in France. He is wounded and gassed

1919 J. B. Priestley is awarded a place at Trinity Hall, Cambridge University, to study literature, history and political science

1922 J. B. Priestley begins work in London as a journalist writing for publications such as *The Times Literary Supplement* and *The New Statesman*. He publishes his first collection of essays under the title *Brief Diversions*

1926 The General Strike hits British industry

1929 The American economy is hit by a slump and the Wall Street Crash

1934 J. B. Priestley uses his travels through the poorer parts of Britain to write *English Journey*

1939–45 Second World War. J. B. Priestley makes regular wartime broadcasts on BBC Radio; his radio talks are published as *Britain Speaks*

1945 J. B. Priestley writes *An Inspector Calls*; Churchill's wartime coalition government resigns; a Labour government is formed under Clement Attlee after a landslide victory in the General Election; atomic bombs are dropped on Japan

PART TWO: PLOT AND ACTION

Plot summary: What happens in *An Inspector Calls*?

REVISION ACTIVITY

- Go through the summary lists below and **highlight** what you think is the **key moment** in each Act.

- Then find each moment in the **text** and **reread** it. Write down **two reasons** why you think each moment is so **important**.

ACT ONE

- The Birling family and Gerald Croft are celebrating Sheila's engagement to Gerald.

- Mr Birling makes pompous speeches outlining his views on the advances in science, new inventions and the relationship between bosses and workers, and saying they should ignore the 'cranks' (p. 10) who claim everybody has a responsibility to care for everybody else.

- The evening is interrupted by the arrival of a police inspector named Goole making enquiries about the suicide of a young woman, Eva Smith.

- Shown a photograph of the girl, Mr Birling admits he employed her in his factory but sacked her for being one of the leaders of a strike for higher wages.

- Sheila and Eric both feel their father has acted harshly, while Gerald supports Mr Birling's claim that he acted reasonably.

- Sheila is shown the photograph and she realises that, driven by jealousy and ill temper, she later had the girl sacked from her job as a shop assistant.

- When Gerald hears the girl changed her name to Daisy Renton, his reaction shows he too has known the girl.

- The Inspector suggests that many people share responsibility for the misery which prompted Eva Smith/Daisy Renton to end her life.

- Left alone with Gerald, Sheila warns him not to try to hide anything from the Inspector.

ACT TWO

Gerald admits he had met Daisy Renton in the spring of the previous year and that she was his mistress for six months.

Sheila is hurt and angry at Gerald's involvement with the girl, yet she feels a certain respect for the openness of his admission.

- Mrs Birling tries to bully the Inspector and to control events.

- Sheila realises that the Inspector's enquiries are well founded, and that her mother might also have had some dealings with the girl.

- While Eric is out of the room, Mrs Birling is forced to admit the girl asked for the help of a charity that she worked for and was refused.

- It is revealed that the girl was pregnant, and Mrs Birling lays the blame for the girl's death on the father of the unborn child.

- There is a suspicion that Eric might have been the father of that unborn child.

ACT THREE

Eric confesses that he got the girl pregnant and that he stole money from his father's firm to support her.

Learning that the girl had appealed to his mother for help and been turned down, Eric blames his mother for the girl's death.

The Inspector makes a dramatic speech about the consequences of the sort of social irresponsibility that Mr Birling was preaching at the end of the dinner.

The Inspector, having shown that each had a part in ruining the girl's life, leaves.

- Between them Gerald and Mr Birling gradually prove that the man was not a real police inspector.

- A telephone call to the Chief Constable establishes there is no Inspector Goole on the police force.

- A telephone call to the Infirmary reveals that there has been no recent suicide.

- Eric and Sheila continue to feel guilty about what they have done, but the others now shrug off any guilt.

- Mr Birling answers the telephone: a young woman has just died on her way to the Infirmary and an inspector is on his way to make enquiries.

Act One, Part 1: The dinner party (pp. 1–7)

SUMMARY

KEY QUOTE

Mrs Birling: 'men with important work to do sometimes have to spend nearly all their time and energy on their business'

❶ The Birling family and Gerald Croft are enjoying a dinner to celebrate the engagement of Gerald to Sheila.

❷ Mr Birling makes a speech congratulating the engaged couple and expressing the hope that their marriage will lead to closer and more profitable links between the firms owned by the Birling and Croft families.

❸ Gerald presents Sheila with an engagement ring.

❹ The ladies leave the room while the men enjoy port and cigars.

WHY IS THIS SECTION IMPORTANT?

A It introduces five of the main **characters**.

B It establishes the **relationships** between those characters.

C It demonstrates the **wealth** and **social position** of the Birling and Croft families.

D It hints at Mr Birling's **attitude** to life in general and marriage in particular.

E It introduces key ideas about **social justice**, **class distinction** and how life will develop in the **future**.

KEY QUOTE

Mr Birling: 'I speak as a hard-headed business man'

THE BIRLING FAMILY – CONTRASTING CHARACTERS

Sheila's light-hearted, excitable and enthusiastic manner is very different from Eric's behaviour. Having drunk too much, Eric lacks control, suddenly laughing, speaking 'rather noisily' (p. 5) and making comments which lead to Sheila calling him 'an ass' (p. 3).

Although the scene centres on the celebration of Sheila's engagement, there are moments which foreshadow later revelations. J. B. Priestley drops in the information that Gerald 'never came near' (p. 3) Sheila the previous summer, which is strange if the couple were so very much in love. Doubts are raised about their love, and about how truthful the characters are, when Sheila responds to Gerald's explanation with 'that's what *you* say' (p. 3), hinting that there might be another explanation.

EXAMINER'S TIP

The examiner will be impressed if you use well-chosen quotations from the play to back up your points – but make sure your quotations are accurate!

Mr Birling enjoys playing the host. We see how his life centres round his business, and he regards his family as another way of increasing his business interests. His background as a local politician is suggested as he can't resist making speeches, but when, in these lengthy monologues, he talks about the future, about peace and prosperity and about 'Capital' and 'Labour' (p. 7) working together, the audience can see that his extreme confidence is misplaced.

Mrs Birling never really enters the general conversation. When she speaks we see a person who is very self-controlled and rather cold. She clearly disapproves of young people drinking, and she places a high value on things being done in what she considers to be the right way.

THE FAMILY'S SOCIAL POSITION – WEALTH AND BUSINESS

The family's wealth is suggested by the formal nature of the dinner party. In his stage directions, J. B. Priestley describes how the set should look so that the family's privileged lifestyle is made clear. The solid furniture, the champagne, port and cigars all reflect a very comfortable lifestyle where luxury is taken for granted. The hard furniture also suggests a lack of family warmth and homeliness, despite the luxury.

The references to business and to the Croft family's higher social standing and greater wealth indicate the things that Mr Birling considers important. Although he comes from a modest background, Mr Birling sees the future wedding of Sheila to Gerald as the beginning of a powerful business empire.

Mr Birling's toast wishing the happy couple 'the very best that life can bring' (p. 4) seems to suggest that they all think it is natural that life should be good to them. J. B. Priestley is preparing us for the contrast we will see between the way of life enjoyed by the wealthy and the hardships endured by those who work for them.

EXAMINER'S TIP: WRITING ABOUT MR BIRLING AND THE SOCIAL CONTEXT OF THE PLAY

This section helps you to examine how J. B. Priestley uses the comfortable view of life enjoyed by the wealthy before the First World War to indicate the ways in which life would change during the twentieth century. Mr Birling is confident that the future will bring good times to factory owners like him, with fewer strikes and greater prosperity. He talks about advances in technology, quoting the newly launched *Titanic* as a symbol of progress. You can show how wrong he is when he declares that by 1940 the world will be a place of peace with wars a thing of the past. Illustrate how we are led to doubt what Mr Birling says later in the play, by how wrong we see him to be in his view of what the future holds. His view that socialist ideas of equality and workers' rights are dangerous will be destroyed when the Inspector shows how much people like Eva Smith need protection.

CHECKPOINT 1

What are our immediate impressions of Mr Birling? Consider the views he expresses.

DID YOU KNOW?

The *Titanic* was owned by the White Star Company. When she was launched she was the largest ship afloat and it was thought she was unsinkable. She sank on her maiden voyage after hitting an iceberg, on 14 April 1912, and 1,500 people lost their lives.

GLOSSARY

Capital Mr Birling uses the word to represent those who owned the factories

Labour Mr Birling refers here to employed working people rather than the political Labour Party

Act One, Part 2: Mr Birling confides in Gerald (pp. 7–11)

SUMMARY

❶ Gerald Croft remains in the dining room with Mr Birling who is worried about what Gerald's mother thinks of the family.

❷ Mr Birling tells Gerald there is a chance of his getting a knighthood in the New Year's Honours list.

❸ Gerald and Mr Birling joke about a scandal ruining that possibility.

❹ Eric returns and tells them the women are talking about clothes so there is no hurry.

❺ Mr Birling states that a man's only responsibility is to himself and his family. He laughs at the notion of responsibility to others in society.

❻ He is interrupted by someone at the front door.

WHY IS THIS SECTION IMPORTANT?

A It allows Mr Birling to **talk** with Gerald while the rest of the family are **not present**.

B It reveals the **selfish** way in which the Birlings and Crofts think.

C Although Mr Birling's **wealth** comes from his own hard work, we learn that he feels **socially inferior** to the Crofts.

D It is revealed that Mr Birling is in line for a **knighthood**.

E There are **hints** about **secrets** which could affect the **characters** in the future.

THE BIRLINGS AND THE CROFTS – AMBITION AND MONEY

It is interesting that, despite his wealth, Mr Birling fears that Lady Croft (Gerald's mother) sees his family as being socially beneath her. He suspects that Lady Croft believes Gerald 'might have done better' (p. 8) by choosing a future wife from a better family. Gerald denies this, leading us to understand that having money is now more important in society than coming from land-owning gentry.

Mr Birling's hope for a knighthood shows that he is someone who is going up in the world. We notice that Mr Birling confides his news to Gerald, allowing Gerald to drop a hint to Lady Croft, although Mr Birling knows that he should keep this news secret until it is officially announced.

Although Mr Birling is happy to benefit from whatever he can take from the community, he ridicules the idea that we might all be 'mixed up together like bees in a hive' (p. 10), living as a community in which everyone looks after each other and works for the common good. As the play progresses, the Inspector brings out the ways in which the Birling family bears responsibility for ruining the girl's life.

KEY QUOTE

Mr Birling: 'a man has to mind his own business and look after himself and his own'

 **DID YOU KNOW?**

Many people in the past bought knighthoods and other honours by making donations to the political party that was in power.

WOMEN AND CLOTHES – THE HAVES AND HAVE NOTS

We see how trivial are the concerns which occupy the Birling women. Eric remarks on the way 'women are potty' about clothes (p. 9). Mr Birling recognises that women see clothes as a status symbol, a 'token of their self-respect' (p. 9).

Later we learn how Sheila's choice of an unsuitable dress amuses the girl in the dress shop. Sheila's position of power will lead to the girl losing her job.

The importance that Mr Birling attaches to his possible knighthood shows us what men in his position feel is necessary to prove their value in society. He knows that there must be no hint of scandal attached to anyone being considered for a reward in the Honours List, but cannot seriously believe that he or his family can be in any danger of that. Consider how the mention of scandal, Eric's slip of the tongue about previous experience with women, and Gerald's joking suggestion that there is something 'a bit fishy' (p. 9) about Eric's past, all hint at some sort of secret that will upset the family.

J. B. Priestley shows us how superficial the honours system can be when being a 'sound useful party man' (p. 8) counts so highly towards gaining Mr Birling his knighthood. It is important to show how Mr Birling is characterised as a hypocrite because he is happy to accept the community's reward of a knighthood while his speech shows that he believes commitment to the community to be nonsense.

Act One, Part 3: The enquiry begins (pp. 11–16)

SUMMARY

❶ An inspector enters the room, but Mr Birling tries to take control, mentioning his long service in local government and his position as a magistrate.

❷ The Inspector is unimpressed and says he has come to make enquiries about a girl who has died in the 'Infirmary' (p. 11) after deliberately drinking disinfectant.

❸ Mr Birling recognises the girl, named Eva Smith, from a photograph which the Inspector produces.

❹ It turns out that Mr Birling sacked the girl for her part in leading a strike for higher wages.

WHY IS THIS SECTION IMPORTANT?

A The **cosy** dinner party **atmosphere** is interrupted by the arrival of the Inspector.

B We see Mr Birling **losing control** of events.

C A **link** is made between the **suicide** of Eva Smith and the Birling family.

D Some very different **attitudes** are revealed.

MR BIRLING AND THE INSPECTOR – A CONTRAST

The Inspector immediately assumes the role of someone who is a force for good. He creates a big impression and seems solid and full of purpose. He has an air of sincerity and takes control of the situation calmy. It is important that he makes an immediate impact because the play is going to be rather more complicated than an ordinary whodunnit.

From being relaxed and rather condescending in his manner, Mr Birling quickly becomes aggressive as he finds himself having to defend his actions. He considers that his importance as a business man, a former 'alderman ... and Lord Mayor' (p. 11) and a local magistrate makes him superior to a mere police inspector. The Inspector stands for the law, and believes that all are equal in the eyes of the law.

THE DEATH OF THE GIRL – CAUSE AND EFFECT

We learn about the way a factory owner might have regarded his workers. Although Eva Smith was a good worker, Mr Birling and Gerald both believe he had to sack her because she had led the factory girls in their request for better pay, and better pay for the workers meant less profit for the factory owner. Eric is seen to have a more sympathetic view, and J. B. Priestley wants us to see things as Eric does.

The Inspector creates the idea of a 'chain of events' (p. 14) leading to Eva Smith's death. This links her to Mr Birling, preparing us for future revelations which will link others to the girl. At the end of this section, by asking about 'what happened to her after that' (p. 16), Mr Birling himself opens the way for such links.

EXAMINER'S TIP: WRITING ABOUT SOCIAL STATUS

Eva Smith does not appear, yet she is central to the developing action of the play. Her diary and letter give the Inspector the information he needs to follow his chain of events. By detailing his record as businessman and local politician, and by referring to friends such as the 'Chief Constable' (p. 16), Mr Birling tries to intimidate the Inspector. The Inspector remains calm and pushes ahead with his questions. We see how Mr Birling looks down on ordinary workers, and he has no loyalty to those who work for him. It is ironic that Mr Birling sacked Eva Smith for showing qualities of leadership – the same qualities for which he was earlier prepared to promote her. J. B. Priestley makes her case through the Inspector. Like Eric, the Inspector is sympathetic towards the girl, and so we feel that J. B. Priestley too is sympathetic towards her. Such sympathy is in clear contrast to the feelings expressed by both Mr Birling and Gerald, the two men of business.

KEY QUOTE

Inspector: 'But after all it's better to ask for the earth than to take it.'

★ **GRADE BOOSTER**

Notice how Mr Birling's views on community and responsibility are interrupted by the Inspector's arrival. This is **ironic** since the Inspector is there to try to teach them about real responsibility.

GLOSSARY

alderman a senior member of a town council

Chief Constable the senior officer in charge of a county or municipal police force

CHECKPOINT 3

What information does the Inspector give us about Eva Smith in Act One?

Act One, Part 4: Sheila's sympathy turns to shock (pp. 16–21)

SUMMARY

❶ When Sheila returns, Mr Birling thinks their business with the Inspector has ended.

❷ The Inspector annoys Mr Birling by continuing his enquiries.

❸ Sheila is shocked by the description of the girl's suicide.

❹ Mr Birling becomes less aggressive when he realises that others in the family might know something of the girl's life.

❺ Sheila becomes agitated on hearing the girl was sacked from Milwards.

❻ Shown a photograph, Sheila runs from the room crying.

KEY QUOTE

Sheila: 'What do you mean by saying that? You talk as if we were responsible – '

WHY IS THIS SECTION IMPORTANT?

A   It **strengthens** the **idea** of a **chain of events**.

B   We realise there is a **link** between Sheila and the girl.

C   We see how both Eric and Sheila feel initial **sympathy** for the girl.

D   Sheila's reaction to the way the girl died increases our sense of **horror**.

E   Mr Birling begins to sense a possible **scandal**, and so the girl's story takes on greater **significance** for the family.

NEW LINKS IN THE CHAIN

Eric is prepared to believe that his father's treatment of the girl two years earlier might have a link to her death, and Sheila sympathises with the girl. She agrees with the Inspector that girls like Eva Smith 'aren't cheap labour – they're *people*' (p. 19). Sheila is drawn in to the girl's tragic story.

Mr Birling begins to take the idea of a scandal more seriously. We are reminded of his conversation with Gerald, and of the way that scandal could put an end to Mr Birling's hopes for a knighthood. We become aware that he is much more concerned with hiding any unpleasantness than with having the truth known; he wants to keep the appearance of respectability.

? DID YOU KNOW?

Before the First World War the majority of working women in the United Kingdom worked as domestic servants. As a factory or shop worker, Eva might have expected to have more freedom.

SHEILA — HER SYMPATHY AND HER GUILT

The Inspector attracts the sympathy of Sheila and of the audience with his clear hard-hitting description of the girl's misery. That sympathy is increased by the details of her pleasant appearance, of the poverty she suffered after losing her job at Birlings and by the absence of relatives to help her when she was in trouble.

Sheila's distress at the girl's suicide is strengthened when she compares the girl's misery with her own happiness that evening. We become aware of the link between Sheila and the shop where the girl found employment, and Sheila's initial distress at having her happy evening spoiled by the sad news serves to reflect the greater unhappiness of the dead girl's life. Sheila's earlier sympathy and sadness make her selfish treatment of the girl in the dress shop seem even more harsh and unjustified when the photograph establishes that link and Sheila has to make her confession.

EXAMINER'S TIP: WRITING ABOUT DRAMATIC EFFECT – THE PHOTOGRAPH

The Inspector uses the photograph to very good effect. It is important that he shows the photograph to only one person at any one time. This means that no one character can ever be sure that they have seen the same photograph as any other character. This adds to the sense of mystery which surrounds both the girl and the Inspector. When the photograph is used, it has an immediate effect on whoever sees it, especially Sheila. We do not need to be told that Sheila was the complaining customer.

Playwrights often use devices which help them to create their plot and manipulate their characters. The girl's diary is never seen but is used to help give the Inspector knowledge about her and the events in her life. The photograph is seen and used, but the way it is used has been criticised by some who see it as an unlikely device, and too convenient. Think about J. B. Priestley's use of the photograph and be prepared to have your own view on this – and be able to give reasons for that view.

GRADE BOOSTER

By commenting on how J. B. Priestley uses the devices of the photograph and diary to build the chain linking all the characters with Eva Smith/ Daisy Renton, you can show an understanding of his ability to create what is known as a well-made play.

CHECKPOINT 4

Pick out some moments in Act One that show the Inspector's power over the other **characters**.

Act One, Part 5: Sheila and the shop girl (pp. 21–6)

SUMMARY

❶ Mr Birling is angry with the Inspector for upsetting Sheila, and he goes out to te[ll] his wife what is happening.

❷ Sheila returns and confesses that she was the customer who had the girl sacked.

❸ The Inspector makes Sheila realise what a terrible thing she has done.

❹ The Inspector reveals the girl had changed her name to Daisy Renton. Gerald reacts sharply to the name.

❺ Sheila warns Gerald not to try to hide the truth.

KEY QUOTE

Inspector: 'A nice little promising life there, I thought, and a nasty mess somebody's made of it.'

WHY IS THIS SECTION IMPORTANT?

A We see Mr Birling's desire to **protect** his daughter.

B The Inspector's position is becoming more **powerful**.

C The family's **involvement** with the girl is revealed.

D We discover more **information** about the girl.

E We see how people can **misuse wealth** and **social status**.

TWO GIRLS – SHEILA AND EVA/DAISY

Mr Birling is more concerned that his daughter has been upset than by any feelings of guilt for what they have done to Eva Smith. Sheila has shown that she can be jealous, petty and spiteful. She used her power as the 'daughter of a good customer' (p. 24) to have the shopgirl sacked. Sheila's description of the girl as pretty and looking 'as if she could take care of herself' (p. 24) shows Sheila's superficial judgement.

We already know something of the family's involvement with the girl and that the Inspector had not come just to see Mr Birling. Gerald's interest in seeing the photograph prepares us for his reaction to hearing she had changed her name to Daisy Renton. He clearly knows the name. We have also been told that the girl had 'decided she might try another kind of life' (p. 23) and we realise what sort of life this was when we hear how Gerald came to meet her.

Sheila's regret seems genuine, and we feel she has learnt a valuable lesson and is determined never to act so unfairly again. When she expresses her wish that she could help the girl now, the Inspector is not gentle with her; he uses three short, sharp sentences: 'Yes, but you can't. It's too late. She's dead' (p. 24).

Towards the end of the section, Sheila realises that Gerald's lack of attention to her the previous summer was because he was having an affair with Daisy Renton. Gerald has to admit the truth, but clearly believes that because he has not seen Daisy for six months he has nothing to do with the Inspector's investigation. Notice how Sheila is beginning to identify with the Inspector's point of view, and how her belief in him leads her to warn Gerald not to try to fool him.

THE INSPECTOR'S POWER

The Inspector is seen as being more and more in command of the situation. He begins giving his opinions more clearly, and his comment 'a nasty mess somebody's made of it' (p. 21) can be linked to his comment 'if it was left to me' (p. 22) to suggest he is setting himself up as a judge. This changes his position, giving him the authority to state that his enquiries are being made so that all concerned might try to understand why the girl had to die.

By letting the Inspector sum up what has so far been revealed about the involvement of Mr Birling and Sheila, J. B. Priestley reminds us of how events are developing. Sheila's hysterical laugh when she warns Gerald, 'Why – you fool – *he knows*. Of course he knows. And I hate to think how much he knows that we don't know yet' (p. 26) shows how she has come under the Inspector's power.

J. B. Priestley tells us that Gerald is 'crushed' (p. 26), and this shows a very different side of him from the self-assured young man we saw at the beginning of the play. When the Inspector returns, his one-word question 'Well?' at the end of Act One (p. 26) raises his position to that of an all-knowing inquisitor. It adds to our sense of mystery as to where the Inspector has got so much detailed knowledge.

EXAMINER'S TIP: WRITING ABOUT THE THEME OF GUILT

Guilt is one of the main themes of this play. When the Inspector quite brutally reminds Sheila that the girl is dead and there is nothing she can do about it we, like Sheila, realise that you cannot go back and change what has happened. Each character in turn is shown a reason why they should feel guilty, but it is important to explore whether or not they admit to their guilt and how they deal with it. Look also at how Priestley manipulates the characters towards the end of the play. After the Inspector has gone they mostly shrug off any sense of guilt for their actions – until, that is, the telephone rings.

An Inspector Calls **19**

KEY QUOTE

Sheila: 'At least I'm trying to tell the truth. I expect you've done things you're ashamed of too.'

GRADE BOOSTER

Make sure you comment on the *effect* of events on the audience. Do they evoke sympathy? Shock? How?

GLOSSARY

crushed defeated

Act Two, Part 1: Sharing the guilt (pp. 27–9)

SUMMARY

❶ Gerald resents the decision that Sheila should stay to hear the details of his involvement with Daisy Renton.

❷ The Inspector says that Sheila has accepted her share of responsibility and needs to hear what else happened to the girl so that she does not feel she is the only one who is to blame.

❸ They agree that sharing something, even blame, is better than not sharing anything.

❹ Mrs Birling comes in.

KEY QUOTE

Inspector: 'And you think young women ought to be protected against unpleasant and disturbing things?'

WHY IS THIS SECTION IMPORTANT?

A The **argument** between Sheila and Gerald reveals a **lack** of real **trust** and **understanding** in their relationship.

B It reveals more of Sheila's sense of **guilt**.

C The Inspector shows that he **understands** how Sheila feels.

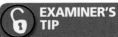

EXAMINER'S TIP

Always read all the relevant parts of the examination paper before you start writing – and that includes the instructions!

SHEILA AND GERALD – THEIR RELATIONSHIP

Gerald's suggestion that Sheila should leave the room because she has had a 'long, exciting and tiring day' (p. 27) suggests that Gerald believes Sheila wants to stay only so that she can see him shamed, just as he saw her shamed. We see his excuse that she should not have to go through something which might be 'unpleasant and disturbing' (p. 27) as being hypocritical since Daisy Renton was not spared what was unpleasant and disturbing for her.

When Gerald accuses Sheila of wanting to see him 'put through it' (p. 28) we realise that he has something terrible to hide. Sheila is shocked, not because Gerald might have been unfaithful to her but because if he can think so badly of her then he cannot really love her. However, we also see that Sheila wants to know that she is not the only one responsible for the girl's death, and that knowing that might be more important to her than anything she might learn about Gerald.

SHEILA'S GUILT – THE INSPECTOR'S INSIGHT

The Inspector does not spare Sheila's feelings. When he again describes Daisy as a 'pretty, lively sort of girl' (p. 28) we are reminded of the comparison between her and Sheila. His description of Daisy and her miserable death adds to Sheila's feelings of guilt.

The Inspector seems to understand Sheila's feelings in a strange, almost unnatural way, and this adds to the mystery which surrounds him. He does not spare her feelings, and his blunt way of describing the circumstances of the girl's death is intended to add to the sense of guilt felt by Sheila and later by Gerald.

EXAMINER'S TIP: WRITING ABOUT SHEILA AND THE INSPECTOR

Notice how Priestley uses shock tactics so that the Inspector's bluntness makes the audience more inclined to condemn those who have mistreated the girl. An interesting point in this section is that although Sheila is clearly upset by what has happened, we begin to sense a bond, a link, forming between her and the Inspector. He understands her need to share the blame, and not to be alone with her guilt 'the rest of tonight, all tomorrow, all the next night – ' (p. 29). He lets Sheila admit her guilt, and admit that she can't bear to feel completely responsible for the girl's death. It is worth pointing out that Sheila is struck by the truth of what the Inspector says, even though she cannot properly understand his power or his nature.

KEY QUOTE

Inspector: 'You see, we have to share something. If there's nothing else, we'll have to share our guilt.'

GRADE BOOSTER

Read and re-read the play so that you become really familiar with the plot, **themes** and **characters**.

Act Two, Part 2: Mrs Birling bustles in (pp. 29–32)

SUMMARY

❶ Mrs Birling suspects that Sheila is motivated only by unhealthy curiosity and has no need to stay and be a part of the enquiry.

❷ She is puzzled when Sheila tries to warn her that the Inspector can break down any defences.

❸ Mrs Birling tries to impress the Inspector by reminding him of her husband's importance in the community.

❹ She is shocked to find that Eric has been regularly drinking far too much.

❺ She accuses Sheila of being the one who is destroying the family's reputation.

WHY IS THIS SECTION IMPORTANT?

A J. B. Priestley shows us a sharp **contrast** between Mrs Birling and Sheila.

B Eric's **problem** with drink is introduced.

C Mrs Birling's **ignorance** of her son's drinking habit, and the way she tries to **bully** the Inspector, show us how **insensitive** she is.

D Sheila's behaviour shows us the Inspector's ability to **control** situations.

MRS BIRLING AND SHEILA – WARNINGS IGNORED

Sheila is quick to realise that her mother is 'beginning all wrong' (p. 29), and as we see Mrs Birling's bold confidence we understand Sheila's concern. Sheila has already begun to make connections between the girl and the family, and she fears that her mother also has a guilty secret concerning her treatment of the girl.

Mrs Birling treats the Inspector with less respect than the others have done, and the **dialogue** between her and the Inspector has the tone of mistress talking to servant. She feels that the Inspector's attitude and questioning are offensive and 'a trifle impertinent' (p. 30). She believes that she cannot be expected to know anything about '[g]irls of that class' (p. 30) and is confident she can handle any questions which are put to her. Her language suggests that she wants to show the Inspector how superior she is.

Sheila is aware that her mother has not yet faced being questioned by the Inspector. Mrs Birling's superior tone when she enters the room is quite out of keeping with the apprehension which Sheila and Gerald share as a result of their feelings of responsibility. We understand Sheila's warnings, and start to wonder what the Inspector will soon reveal about Mrs Birling.

When Mrs Birling tells the Inspector that he seems to have 'made a great impression on this child' (p. 30) we suspect that she doesn't see Sheila as being fully grown up. She feels that while the Inspector can impress a 'child', he cannot have any effect on someone like her. Mrs Birling brings up Mr Birling's respected position in the community, and Gerald's warning that it is not a good idea to remind the Inspector of that brings us back to Mr Birling's fear of a scandal.

ERIC – A YOUNG MAN WITH A PROBLEM

Sheila has to tell her mother about Eric's problem with drink. Because she has already confessed about her behaviour towards the girl, it is easier for Sheila to do this, especially because Gerald gently supports what she has said.

Notice the way that we are gradually given more information about Eric and his drinking. In Act One he has drunk more than he should during the dinner. Sheila describes him as being 'squiffy' (p. 3), a slang expression which seems quite humorous, although Mrs Birling appears to be shocked by it. Now we learn that he has a reputation as someone who 'does drink very hard' (p. 32). This prepares us for the later revelations about his drunken behaviour towards the girl. It is like a second, smaller, chain of events.

EXAMINER'S TIP: WRITING ABOUT WORDS AND IMAGES

Think about how J. B. Priestley uses the image of a wall to show Sheila's empathy. Sheila suggests that when we are guilty we defend ourselves with a wall of self-belief. When the wall is knocked down we feel even more vulnerable. Sheila does not doubt that the Inspector can knock down any defences that Mrs Birling will put up.

You can also highlight J. B. Priestley's pointed play on words when the word 'offence' (p. 31) is repeated twice in the dialogue between Mrs Birling and the Inspector. At first it is used to suggest the possibility of someone being offended, but then there is also the suggestion of the law having been broken and a criminal offence having taken place.

KEY QUOTE

Inspector: 'he's a young man. And some young men drink far too much.'

GLOSSARY

squiffy slightly drunk

impertinent cheeky

CHECKPOINT 5

How does Gerald's confession contrast with Mr Birling's earlier unwillingness to accept any blame?

Act Two, Part 3: Gerald's confession (pp. 32–40)

SUMMARY

❶ Mr Birling, who has been trying to persuade Eric to go to bed, is further annoyed by the Inspector's insistence on doing things his own way.

❷ Gerald makes a feeble attempt to deny any link with the girl.

❸ He then admits he had met the girl and she had become his mistress.

WHY IS THIS SECTION IMPORTANT?

A The Inspector brings out the **connection** between Gerald and the girl, Daisy Renton.

B We see both Gerald and the girl in a **different way**.

C Gerald and Sheila are made to look **afresh** at their own **relationship**.

KEY QUOTE

Inspector: 'As soon as I mentioned the name Daisy Renton, it was obvious you'd known her.'

EXAMINER'S TIP

When you have jotted down all the points you wish to use in your examination or coursework essay, take time to organise them carefully.

GERALD – A GOOD MAN DOING THE WRONG THING?

J. B. Priestley is careful that the men use **euphemistic** language such as 'Daisy Renton with other ideas' (p. 33) and 'women of the town' (p. 34) to imply prostitution. People would have had to do this in 1912 so as not offend the ladies.

When Gerald sees Daisy in the bar of the Palace music hall, or theatre, he clearly recognises that she is out of place. Gerald's description of the unattractive 'hard-eyed, dough-faced women' (p. 34) emphasises Daisy's prettiness and her vulnerability. As a result, we are more likely to blame Gerald for what happens, even though we can appreciate his motives for rescuing her from Alderman Meggarty. The mention of the Alderman, a senior local Councillor, shows that anyone can become mixed up in scandalous behaviour. It is a warning to Mr Birling.

As the Inspector tells Gerald how, after he had ended the relationship, the girl went away 'to be alone, to be quiet, to remember all that had happened' (p. 39), we see that Gerald had brought something pleasant and memorable into the girl's sad life – although she probably placed more importance on the relationship than he did.

GERALD AND SHEILA – A CHANGING RELATIONSHIP

Gerald's honest confession adds to our knowledge of when things happened to Eva Smith/Daisy Renton. It also makes him a more sympathetic character. He had tried to help the girl, and had not set out to have an affair with her.

Sheila is understandably upset when she learns of Gerald's relationship with the girl. She becomes increasingly sarcastic with Gerald, whom she calls 'the hero' (p. 34) of the story they are listening to, and later she tries to ridicule him saying the girl saw him as 'the wonderful Fairy prince' (p. 38). This is her way of coping with the revelations about him, but it might also suggest her own feelings for Gerald as well as showing that life with Gerald could only be a fantasy for a girl like Daisy.

Towards the end of this section, Sheila's attitude towards Gerald has softened again. By accepting her own blame for having the girl sacked from the shop, and by accepting Gerald's good intentions when he first saw the girl, Sheila sees events in a different way. She returns the engagement ring because she feels that she and Gerald are only just beginning to get to know each other. Both she and Gerald show they are prepared to start over again, and this holds out hope for their future.

EXAMINER'S TIP: WRITING ABOUT THE INSPECTOR – A MAN WHO KNOWS

The purpose of this section is to make us more aware of the Inspector's ability to ask very simple questions and yet to obtain a great deal of information. The Inspector has already used the photograph to establish the girl's identity, and it is important that you realise how the 'rough sort of diary' (p. 39) provides Priestley with a convenient device to explain the Inspector's close knowledge of events. Together with the characters, we too become impressed by how much the Inspector knows, and we begin to see how far-sighted Sheila was when she said 'Of course he knows. And I hate to think how much he knows that we don't know yet' (p. 26).

Sheila's words can be viewed as making the Inspector appear a more powerful and knowing character. As the play progresses, make notes on the way he changes from a plodding police officer doing a simple job of making enquiries about a suicide, into a symbol of righteous vengeance, someone who stands for what is right and good, who will not tolerate hypocrisy and who will avenge the wrongs done to those who are weak and helpless.

CHECKPOINT 6

How has Gerald's confession affected Sheila's feelings about him?

Act Two, Part 4: Sheila warns her mother (pp. 40–2)

SUMMARY

① When Sheila comments that Gerald was not shown the photograph, the Inspector points out that it was unnecessary.

② He shows the photograph to Mrs Birling.

③ She claims that she does not recognise the girl, and she is angry when the Inspector says that she is lying.

④ Mr Birling demands an apology from the Inspector who, instead of apologising, points out that power and influence bring 'responsibilities as well as privileges' (p. 41).

⑤ Sheila advises her mother to tell the truth and not to make things worse.

⑥ The front door slams and Mr Birling goes to see if Eric has left the house.

WHY IS THIS SECTION IMPORTANT?

A Through **Sheila** we are shown more of the Inspector's **power** to reveal the family's **dark secrets**.

B We again have a summary of the **links** in the **chain**.

C We see that Mr Birling and his wife feel they are **shielded** by their **social position**.

KEY QUOTE

Sheila: 'we've no excuse now for putting on airs and if we've any sense we won't try.'

EXAMINER'S TIP

Remember to refer to the text as a play – don't call it the book!

SHEILA – A CHARACTER WHO SEES THE TRUTH

Sheila is aware that they must not try to hide from what they have done. It is clear that she believes her mother has something to hide, and that if her mother tries to hide it she will only be 'making it worse' (p. 42) and she will be sorry in the end.

It seems that Sheila is the only one who appreciates the Inspector's power to reveal secrets they have never even realised were hidden. The Inspector has come to find out who was to blame for the girl's suicide, and Sheila's summary of events reminds us of the greed, jealousy and selfishness they have shown.

Mr Birling and his wife still try to use their respected place in the community to remind the Inspector of his relatively humble social status. Sheila clearly believes that social status has nothing to do with what is happening that evening, and her advice to her mother that she might as well admit being involved in the Brumley Women's Charity Organization can be seen as advice that she might as well admit whatever involvement she had with the girl.

THE CHAIN – A FURTHER REMINDER

erald was not shown the photograph. His reaction to the girl's name was enough to how recognition. When Mrs Birling is shown the photograph she denies recognising e face that she sees, but the Inspector is not afraid to call her bluff and we mmediately believe him and not her.

s Sheila reminds us that Mr Birling sacked Eva Smith for asking for a reasonable age, and that she herself had the girl fired from the shop because she was jealous f her, our sympathy for the girl increases. When we are reminded of how Gerald ok her as his mistress and then dropped her, we again see how badly life, and the rlings, have treated the girl.

heila is used by J. B. Priestley to remind us of the way Mr Birling, Sheila and Gerald ad mistreated the girl. This strengthens our confidence in the truth of the spector's accusations and in his knowledge. The more times the chain of events is peated, the more our belief in it grows and the more faith we have in the spector.

GRADE BOOSTER

Embed your quotations in your own sentences. Always try to use short quotations which help you to make your point precisely.

EXAMINER'S TIP: WRITING ABOUT SOCIAL STATUS

It is important to understand that, in 1912, social position was very much dictated by a person's family connections or wealth. The Birlings belong to the important, wealthy group of people who would expect to run things in a town like Brumley. A Police Inspector was regarded rather like a servant of such people, but Inspector Goole shows no fear of Mr Birling's importance in the town. He takes the moral high ground, reminding Mr Birling that men who hold public office 'have responsibilities as well as privileges' (p. 41). Consider how, by emphasising the ideas of duty and responsibility, the Inspector suggests the family's lack of such qualities. It makes us question their 'right' to consider themselves superior to working people such as the Inspector and the girl.

CHECKPOINT 7

In what ways does Eric fit the description of the father of the unborn child?

Act Two, Part 5: The deserving and the undeserving (pp. 42–9)

SUMMARY

① Mr Birling returns with the news that Eric has left the house.

② Mrs Birling admits she is a member of the Brumley Women's Charity Organizatio□ which was set up to help 'women in distress' (p. 42).

③ The Organization's committee interviewed the girl two weeks ago.

④ Mrs Birling was responsible for the girl being refused help.

⑤ Mrs Birling tells her version of what the girl told the committee.

KEY QUOTE

Mrs Birling: 'that was one of the things that prejudiced me against her case.'

EXAMINER'S TIP

Think about the way **characters** are gradually revealed, and make lists of important moments and quotations to help with your revision.

WHY IS THIS SECTION IMPORTANT?

A It **reveals** Mrs Birling's **link** to the girl.

B It shows us the family's **different reactions** to events.

C We see the Inspector as a sort of **prosecutor** and **judge** combined.

D The girl's **pregnancy** is revealed for the first time.

E Mrs Birling's insistence that **blame** for the girl's **death** rests with the unborn child's father leads to the **dramatic** ending of the Act.

MRS BIRLING – AN UNCHARITABLE CHARITY WORKER

We are brought almost up-to-date with the girl's story when we learn that Mrs Birling saw her only two weeks before her death. We would expect the members of the Brumley Women's Charity Organization to be gentle, caring and sympathetic towards women in trouble. It is clear that Mrs Birling showed none of these qualitie□

Mrs Birling has a strong sense of how people of different classes should behave. Her prejudice towards the girl seems based on a belief that an unmarried working-class girl who has become pregnant could never behave in a noble way – which is what the girl may be said to have done when she refused to take money from the child's father because the money was stolen.

Mrs Birling's prejudice and dislike of the girl's manner echo Mr Birling's attitude when he said 'She'd had a lot to say – far too much – so she had to go' (p. 15) and Sheila's anger because the girl had been 'very impertinent' (p. 24). Each had used their power and position to harm the girl.

THE BIRLINGS – THEIR CAUSES FOR CONCERN

Mrs Birling is anxious to prove she behaved in a reasonable way. To remove any blame from herself, she insists that the girl told lies, including using the name Mrs Birling, and so was not what would have been called a 'deserving' poor person. She states that the father of the unborn child is to blame for what has happened, and she uses his immoral behaviour in fathering the child and his theft of money to show his guilt.

Mr Birling is worried that his wife had seen the girl so recently. He is angry when he learns that the girl had applied to the Brumley Women's Charity Organization using the name 'Mrs Birling'. Mr Birling is relieved once he has made sure that the child wasn't Gerald Croft's, but his wife's treatment of the girl's application for help worries him. Once again, his concern is only that there might be a scandal when the story is revealed at the inquest.

Sheila's reaction to her mother's involvement with the girl shows genuine concern. She is shocked by her mother's defiant admission that she was prejudiced against the girl. When the Inspector mentions the girl's body in the Infirmary we see how Sheila's vivid imagination has enabled her to visualise the sad scene. The news that the girl was pregnant, and so an innocent unborn child has also died, fills Sheila with horror.

KEY QUOTE

Mrs Birling: 'Unlike the other three, I did nothing I'm ashamed of or that won't bear investigation.'

★ **GRADE BOOSTER**

Always read the question carefully. Look for words such as 'examine', 'contrast' or 'compare' so that you can make an appropriate response.

CHECKPOINT 8

How do Mrs Birling's attitude and language affect our view of her?

EXAMINER'S TIP: WRITING ABOUT DRAMATIC EFFECT

It is important that you write about how J. B. Priestley gradually drops in clues which allow the audience to guess, through Sheila, where the chain of events is leading. Although Mrs Birling has seen the girl recently, there is a gap in time between Gerald's affair with the girl and Mrs Birling's encounter with her. The girl's use of the name 'Mrs Birling', the description we are given of the child's father and the fact that Eric, who has gone out for a while, is the only one not yet questioned – all give Sheila clues about what is going to happen. This section is important for the dramatic effect Priestley creates since Sheila is unable to prevent her mother from demanding that the Inspector find the young man and makes sure 'that he's compelled to confess in public his responsibility' (p. 48). Notice how all this builds to the Inspector's calm statement that he is waiting to do that, and to Sheila's final outburst just before Eric makes his entrance.

Act Three, Part 1: Eric in the spotlight (pp. 50–2)

SUMMARY

❶ Eric realises that they all suspect he had some involvement with the girl.

❷ Eric admits that he met the girl at the Palace bar the previous November.

❸ He starts to tell his story and Mrs Birling is shocked and upset by what he says.

❹ Mr Birling insists that Sheila take her mother out to the drawing room.

WHY IS THIS SECTION IMPORTANT?

A It brings out Eric's **relationship** with the girl.

B It fills **gaps** in the girl's **history**.

C Mrs Birling loses her **battle** with the Inspector.

D The Inspector achieves **complete control**.

ERIC – HIS PROBLEM WITH DRINK

As soon as Eric enters, he realises that they all 'know' (p. 50) what he has done. This shows how guilty he must feel. His reaction to the news that his parents know about his heavy drinking is not that of a mature adult. He becomes upset and doesn't realise that Sheila told them to make things easier for him when the truth comes out.

Eric's request for a drink, and the Inspector's insistence that he be allowed a drink, show us how dependent Eric is on alcohol. This little incident shows the even-handed way that the Inspector treats people. Eric sees a drink as something to help him overcome his problems, when it is really the cause of his troubles. The fact that neither of his parents had known about his heavy drinking also shows the weakness of the relationships within the family.

As Eric's guilt is brought out we see the unpleasant nature of his relationship with the girl. He explains how he insisted on going with her to where she lived, forced his way in and had sex with her. He is careful how he describes what he did and simply says 'that's when it happened' (p. 52). Eric's brutish behaviour is closely connected with his excessive drinking. He is shown in an unsympathetic way, and we are again steered towards taking the girl's side.

THE GIRL'S STORY — SOME GAPS ARE FILLED

Both Gerald and Eric met the girl in the bar of the Palace Theatre. Gerald had broken off their relationship in September, and we know that she then went away for a couple of months to enjoy her good memories. Eric meets her in November. He is already slightly drunk, or 'squiffy' (p. 51) and even though he realises she 'wasn't the usual sort' (p. 51) he buys her drinks and insists on going home with her. Unlike Gerald, Eric treats her like a prostitute.

The time gap between Gerald leaving Daisy and Eric meeting her is neatly filled by the Inspector's information about the girl spending two months at the seaside. The money she had from Gerald has run out and so she again tries the way of life from which Gerald had rescued her. When she gives in to Eric, we see that after her affair with Gerald, the girl has resigned herself to adopting the life of the 'women of the town'.

EXAMINER'S TIP: WRITING ABOUT HOW THE INSPECTOR WINS CONTROL

Notice how the Inspector has been gradually gaining control of the situation. He even feels sufficiently confident to overrule Mr Birling and insist that Eric has a drink.

As each character has been questioned they have broken down for one reason or another. Mrs Birling has provided stiffer opposition than the others, but now we see her finally overcome. Her self-confidence showed signs of cracking at the end of Act Two, and Eric's confession starts to make it crumble. She has to leave the room.

KEY QUOTE

Inspector: 'There'll be plenty of time, when I've gone, for you all to adjust your family relationships.'

GRADE BOOSTER

Keep your language formal. Avoid using slang or colloquial language. A formal essay needs formal language.

Act Three, Part 2: A baby on the way (pp. 52–3)

SUMMARY

❶ Eric relates how he met the girl again two weeks later.

❷ He describes their meetings and how the girl told him that she was pregnant.

❸ He gave her money, but then she refused to accept any more.

❹ Mr Birling questions his son about where he had obtained the money.

❺ Eric admits he had taken it from his father's office.

❻ Sheila and Mrs Birling come back into the room.

WHY IS THIS SECTION IMPORTANT?

A   It provides more **details** of Eric's relationship with the girl.

B   We learn more about the **stolen money**.

C   There is a **directness** in **speech** now that the ladies have left the room.

D   The girl is shown to be even more of a **victim** of the family.

ERIC — BRUTISH BEHAVIOUR

Eric's first encounter with the girl is very different from Gerald's, and his later meetings with her seem cold and uncaring. Eric's account of how he met the girl again, and of how he had told her his name but had learnt very little about her, suggests there was little real communication between them. Eric admits he wasn't in love with her, although he liked her. His reasons for liking her, that she 'was pretty and a good sport' (p. 52), are shallow. His relationship with her is a purely physical one and something he sees as a game, a bit of fun.

Eric's admission that the girl didn't want to marry him and that he felt that she treated him like a child, shows that despite his good education and his privileged upbringing he was immature. This is shown again when we learn how he obtained the money which he gave to the girl.

LANGUAGE — NOT IN FRONT OF THE LADIES

Gerald was careful earlier to use expressions such as 'women of the town' (p. 34) so as not to offend the ladies. Eric avoids saying he had sex with the girl by simply saying 'that's when it happened' (p. 52), and Mr Birling has done what he can to prevent his wife and daughter hearing anything unsavoury.

Once the women have left the room the Inspector feels free to ask if Eric and the girl 'made love' (p. 52), and Mr Birling asks if Eric 'had to go to bed with her' (p. 52). These are still **euphemisms**, but in 1912 this was strong language.

Eric is even more free in his speech. He suggests that as a bachelor he is free to associate with the women some of his father's 'respectable friends' (p. 52) are seen with, and he refers to the women as 'fat old tarts' (p. 52) – an expression he would never use in his mother's presence. There is hypocrisy in the way the men regard women.

EXAMINER'S TIP: WRITING ABOUT THE GIRL — EVA SMITH/DAISY RENTON/"MRS BIRLING"

Notice how Priestley delicately avoids any direct reference as to why the girl returned to the bar of the Palace Theatre, but we are led to believe that she was out of work and in desperate need of money. It is important to understand that she has changed: she had been unable to accept the approaches of Alderman Meggarty, but now she has to accept Eric's drunken advances.

Since Eric, the father of her child, has told her his name, it may be seen as quite natural for her to use his name when applying for help from the Brumley Women's Charity Organization. This is a useful point because, combined with her unwillingness to accept stolen money, it makes Mrs Birling's refusal to help her seem even more petty and unjust. You could think also about the effect that her use of the name Mrs Birling has and how differently she might have been treated if she was actually a member of that family.

Consider how the details of the girl are vague. Eric does not even mention her name. This uncertainty about her identity is convenient later on in the play when her very existence is questioned.

Act Three, Part 3: 'Fire and blood and anguish' (pp. 53–6)

SUMMARY

❶ Mr Birling tells his wife that Eric was responsible for the girl's pregnancy and has stolen money from the office.

❷ Mr Birling begins to plan how he can cover up Eric's fraud.

❸ Eric is told of Mrs Birling's part in the story and he accuses his mother of killing her own grandchild.

❹ The Inspector points out how each of them helped to push the girl towards suicide

❺ Before leaving them, the Inspector warns of what will happen if people do not accept that they must live responsibly as part of a caring community.

KEY QUOTE

Inspector: 'One Eva Smith has gone – but there are millions and millions and millions of Eva Smiths and John Smiths still left with us.'

 **DID YOU KNOW?**

J. B. Priestley knew about the 'fire and blood and anguish' (p. 56) of war. He was a soldier in the First World War: some of his experiences are described in his autobiography, *Margin Released*.

WHY IS THIS SECTION IMPORTANT?

A Eric's behaviour marks him as a **thief**, a **criminal**.

B Mr Birling's reaction shows his main concern is once again to **avoid scandal**.

C The **guilt** of each member of the family has been demonstrated.

D The Inspector becomes the **voice of good**.

E The mood of **celebration** we saw at the start of the play is totally **destroyed**.

SCANDAL – REPUTATION AND HONOUR

When Eric reveals his fraud, Mr Birling is immediately aware of the risk of scandal. We are reminded of the joking conversation he had with Gerald early in the play, and we see that what they thought of as humorous and impossible is in fact very possible and very serious. Mr Birling's hopes for a knighthood will be ruined if news of Eric's behaviour gets out. What Eric has done is bound to be discovered when people who have paid their bills in cash to Eric receive a bill showing that they still owe the money. To avoid this, Mr Birling must cover up what Eric has done. He too is prepared to behave dishonestly.

Despite Mr Birling's earlier claims that they are respectable people who have nothing to be ashamed of, we see that Eric could not turn to his father for help when he most needed it. Mr Birling is 'not the kind of father a chap could go to when he's in trouble' (p. 54). The girl finds out that Mrs Birling is not the kind of woman that a girl could turn to when in trouble, despite the fact that the girl's trouble has been made worse by her attempts to protect Eric and her refusal to take money she knew was stolen by Mrs Birling's son.

THE LINKS IN THE CHAIN – GUILT ESTABLISHED

The Inspector has now questioned each of the characters. His repetition of what each has done to harm the girl is a useful reminder of their weaknesses. It shows that the Inspector's job is nearly over. Like the **characters**, we in the audience are left to think back on the part each has played in the girl's death. Only Gerald, who is not present at this time, gets some credit for giving the girl affection and happiness.

The Inspector has not laid blame specifically on any one character. We have seen that as a family they don't really share much, and this takes us back to the Inspector's words, 'we have to share something. If there's nothing else, we'll have to share our guilt' (p. 29). J. B. Priestley, through the Inspector, is now able to make a bold **polemic** statement about every person's responsibility in society.

EXAMINER'S TIP: WRITING ABOUT THE INSPECTOR'S FINAL SPEECH

We can say that the Inspector's final speech has a powerful **didactic** message, which is that we all have some responsibility for looking after one another. Compare it with Mr Birling's speeches in Act One where he proclaims that from his experience 'a man has to mind his own business and look after himself and his own' (p. 10).

Notice that the Inspector warns of future trouble, so there is something of the prophet in the way he speaks, suggesting he is more than an ordinary police inspector. You should point out that J. B. Priestley seems to be preaching, putting forward his own ideas about moral responsibility, about the right that every human being has to be treated fairly. Some critics suggest that he should not have included this sermon-like speech, and should have trusted the play to carry his message. You should form your own opinion about this.

GRADE BOOSTER

Familiarise yourself with technical and literary terms and use them in your answers.

KEY QUOTE

Inspector: 'the time will soon come when, if men will not learn that lesson, then they will be taught it in fire and blood and anguish.'

CHECKPOINT 9

How do the different characters view the importance of the Inspector's status as a police officer?

Act Three, Part 4: A lesson not learnt (pp. 57–61)

SUMMARY

❶ The family argue about what has happened.

❷ Mr Birling is worried that he will not get his knighthood if there is a scandal.

❸ Sheila is very interested when she learns exactly when the Inspector arrived.

❹ Sheila begins to wonder if he was a real police officer.

❺ They believe that if he is not a real police officer a scandal might be avoided.

❻ Gerald returns.

KEY QUOTE

Sheila: 'But now you're beginning all over again to pretend that nothing much has happened.'

WHY IS THIS SECTION IMPORTANT?

A It shows that even when their **guilt** is established the **family** are still **divided**.

B **Questions** are raised about the Inspector's **true identity**.

C A distinct **contrast** is established between the way the two **younger** members of the family and the two **older** ones **react**.

THE BIRLINGS – A FAMILY DIVIDED

Once the Inspector leaves the family turn on each other. It seems that the Inspector's words have not changed the way some of them think. Mr Birling clearly feels that Eric is the only one who has behaved in a way which might be seen as directly causing the girl's death. It is not surprising that Eric feels the responsibilty is shared equally by them all. Eric's attitude takes us back to the Inspector's 'chain of events' (p. 14) which is also, of course, a chain of characters.

? DID YOU KNOW?

During the Second World War, J. B. Priestley was recruited into a top secret unit known as the 'Scallywags', and trained to conduct guerrilla warfare in the event of an enemy invasion.

heila is dismayed by the attitudes shown by her father and mother. Mrs Birling eclares that she had not been intimidated by the Inspector who 'didn't make me onfess – as you call it' (p. 60) while Mr Birling claims the younger ones had 'allowed them]selves to be bluffed' (p. 60) as if they had been playing a game.

uring this section of the play both Eric and Sheila seem more willing and able to tand up to their father. Mrs Birling notices this and accuses them of wanting to help he Inspector instead of them.

KEY QUOTE

Sheila: 'The point is, you don't seem to have learnt anything.'

THE INSPECTOR – INSPECTOR WHO?

becomes clear that they have all noticed something strange about the Inspector. is arrival, just as Mr Birling was making his speech about a man looking after imself, now seems remarkably well timed. When Sheila states that 'he never seemed ke an ordinary police inspector' (p. 59) we are reminded of how all-knowing he eemed. This is strengthened by Sheila's assertion that they 'hardly ever told him nything he didn't know' (p. 60).

heila has been puzzled by the Inspector's knowledge, firmness and concern for the irl. These things mean nothing to her parents who see his behaviour as odd only ecause he failed to show them the respect they expected and had been 'rude – and ssertive' (p. 59).

s far as Sheila is concerned it is not who the Inspector is that is important; it is what e has achieved. She goes over their treatment of the girl, and her conclusion that it is what they did that is important, not whether they admitted it to a real police inspector, quickly refuted by her parents who are concerned about their reputation, not the ate of the girl. To Mr and Mrs Birling the possibility that he might be an imposter is xciting because only a real police officer could take action against them.

GRADE BOOSTER

Remember that a play is intended to be performed and heard, not just read. If you can, go to a theatre production of the play you are studying, or find a television, radio or film version that you can buy or borrow from your local library.

EXAMINER'S TIP: WRITING ABOUT THE TWO GENERATIONS

An important point in this section is that Sheila has faced the truth about herself and her actions rather better than her parents have done. She is amazed and disappointed that there has been no real change in their attitudes. Like Eric she sees no importance in whether the Inspector was a real police officer or not. For her the important thing is that his visit should make them think about, and accept, their responsibilities.

You should notice that, by contrast, Mr Birling sees their confessions as rash and weak behaviour. He can excuse his own admissions since he feels he sacked the girl for what anyone would accept as good business reasons. Mrs Birling simply returns to her claim that she did nothing wrong.

By showing these differences between the generations, J. B. Priestley is suggesting that if after the Second World War society was to change for the better and become fairer (something that failed to happen after the First World War), then the younger generation must be looked to in order to make such changes. It seems in the play that it is the young who are 'more impressionable' (p. 30) and so more likely to take up the ideas of justice and responsibility Priestley puts forward.

CHECKPOINT 10

How do their reactions at this point in the play make Sheila and Eric different from the others?

Act Three, Part 5: Three telephone calls (pp. 61–72)

SUMMARY

❶ Mr and Mrs Birling keep Sheila from telling Gerald about the involvement of Eric and Mrs Birling.

❷ Gerald says a local police sergeant has told him there is no Inspector Goole.

❸ Mr Birling telephones his friend, the Chief Constable, who confirms their suspicio that there is no Inspector Goole.

❹ Gerald telephones the Infirmary, and learns that no one has been taken there after drinking disinfectant.

❺ Gerald tries to persuade Sheila to take back the ring, but she needs time to think.

❻ The telephone rings, and Mr Birling is told that a police inspector is on his way to the house to make enquiries about a young girl's suicide.

KEY QUOTE

Mr Birling: 'I'll admit that fellow's antics rattled us a bit. But we've found him out – and all we have to do is keep our heads.'

WHY IS THIS SECTION IMPORTANT?

A There is a likelihood that Inspector Goole is **not** a real **police officer**.

B **Doubts** are cast as to whether the family had dealings with the **same girl**.

C There is a **lowering** of **tension** because it seems there has been **no suicide** and so **no guilt**.

D The **attitude** of Eric and Sheila is **contrasted** with that of the **other three**.

E We are led towards the **dramatic** final telephone call.

DID YOU KNOW?

An article by J. B. Priestley in the November 1957 issue of the magazine *The New Statesman* led to the formation of the Campaign for Nuclear Disarmament, known as CND.

THE GIRL — WAS SHE THE SAME GIRL?

Gerald brings some proof that the Inspector is not a member of the local police force, and Mr Birling uses his connections to make sure of that. Once doubt is cast on the Inspector's identity, it is natural that the family should start to question the whole story about a girl who is driven to suicide in a chain of events which links all of them.

When Eric says that they 'all helped to kill her' (p. 65) Gerald takes the lead. He uses the uncertainty about the girl's name. He also raises the point that no one else saw the photograph shown to any one character. Putting these ideas together, Gerald leads them to conclude that there might have been several different girls.

The **characters** become excited by the possibility that there was not just one girl, and so there may not have been any suicide. Once again, it is Gerald who thinks of phoning the Infirmary. As an audience we are led to believe that the Inspector's enquiries have been a trick, 'a lot of moonshine. Nothing but an elaborate sell!' (p. 70).

THE YOUNG AND THE OLD — TWO VIEWS OF EVENTS

Mr and Mrs Birling join Gerald in trying to improve their situation by discrediting the Inspector. Several times they congratulate Gerald on his good work. Although he is close in age to Eric and Sheila, Gerald's own position in business is reflected in the way he is seen to be on the same side as Mr Birling.

Gerald, Mr Birling and Mrs Birling see themselves as free of any guilt. Mr Birling even puts forward the idea that it might be a trick thought up by a business rival – business is the only really important thing to him. All three of them quickly accept the idea of a trick, which reduces the seriousness of the admissions they have made.

Eric and Sheila take a rather different view. They do not share the relief felt by the others. They have been so deeply affected by the evening's events that the truth of the Inspector's identity makes no difference to them. Whether it was the same girl they mistreated or two different girls, for Eric and Sheila the guilt and shame remain the same. These two younger characters accept they have done wrong and they cannot easily forget what they have done.

EXAMINER'S TIP: WRITING ABOUT THE PLAY AS A PIECE OF PURE THEATRE

This play relies upon keeping the audience in suspense and slowly letting them in on a little more of the story, suggesting different people who might be responsible for the girl's death. As often happens in thriller plays, films or books, every time we think we have an answer something happens to make us change our minds. Think about how a good play needs to create a lessening of tension before giving the audience a surprise. Notice how, near the end of the play, the dangers to the characters seem to have vanished but, just as they think that all is well, the telephone call changes things back again by reopening the question of the Inspector's identity. It also suggests that the family will have to face the ordeal of questions all over again. It leaves the audience wondering whether it will be the same Inspector who comes to question them and how events will progress this time. The final telephone call was described by one critic as 'the best **coup de théâtre** of the year'.

EXAMINER'S TIP

Always plan your essay. Never start writing until you know what conclusion you intend to reach and how you intend to develop your argument.

KEY QUOTE

Eric: 'You're beginning to pretend now that nothing's really happened at all. And I can't see it like that.'

KEY CONNECTION

If you want to explore J. B. Priestley's time theories further, you might like to read his plays *I Have Been Here Before* and *Time and the Conways*.

Progress and revision check

REVISION ACTIVITY

❶ Why has the Inspector called on the Birling family? (Write your answers below)

....

❷ Why is Mr Birling so afraid of a scandal?

....

❸ What happens when Sheila is shown the photograph of the girl?

....

❹ Where had both Gerald and Eric met the girl?

....

❺ How did Eric obtain the money which he gave Daisy?

....

REVISION ACTIVITY

On a piece of paper write down the answers to these questions:

● Compare Mr Birling's speech to Eric and Gerald (Act One, pp. 9–10) with the Inspector's final speech (Act Three, p. 56).
Start: *Mr Birling shows he has strong views about ...*

● Why might we think Gerald less guilty of harming the girl than the others?
Start: *Unlike the others, Gerald sets out to help the girl ...* or *When Gerald first sees the girl ...*

GRADE BOOSTER

Answer this longer question about the plot of the play:

Q: In what ways does each of the Birling family and Gerald form part of 'a chain of events'? Think about ...

● The contact each has with the girl.

● The way the Inspector questions the characters.

● The timeline of the events brought out by the questioning.

For a C grade: Convey your ideas clearly and appropriately (you could use words from the question to guide your answer) and refer to details from the text.

For an A grade: Make sure you comment on the varied ways the plot is structured, and if possible come up with your own original or alternative ideas. For example, explore the extent to which the play is modelled on conventional detective thrillers.

The Inspector

WHO IS THE INSPECTOR?

He introduces himself as Inspector Goole, a police officer who has come to investigate the background to a young woman's suicide.

WHAT DOES THE INSPECTOR DO IN THE PLAY?

The Inspector interrupts the Birling family gathering.
He establishes they each did something cruel or unkind to the dead girl.
He gradually takes control of the situation and, while being polite, refuses to acknowledge that any of the others is superior to himself.
He leaves them after making an impassioned speech about social justice.

HOW IS THE INSPECTOR DESCRIBED AND WHAT DOES IT MEAN?

Quotation	Means?
A man of 'massiveness, solidity and purposefulness' (p. 11)	The Inspector is an imposing figure who will dominate the play and will achieve his aims.
'One person and one line of enquiry at a time. Otherwise there's a muddle.' (p. 12)	He wants to do things his way, and he likes to do things in an orderly way. This allows J. B. Priestley to build the play as a 'chain of events'.
'It's my duty to ask questions.' (p. 15)	He takes his responsibilities seriously, and shows the others that they haven't done so.
'He never seemed like an ordinary police inspector – ' (p. 59)	The word 'ordinary' could mean 'usual', or it could mean that he was somehow 'extraordinary', more than human.

EXAMINER'S TIP: WRITING ABOUT THE INSPECTOR

Look closely at key words. The word 'inspector' suggests someone who looks closely at things, and this is his role in the play. His name also sounds like ghoul, someone with a morbid interest in death, and it could be said that the Inspector's existence is a result of the girl's death. He remains solid and intact as the others break down, and nothing distracts him from his purpose. He acts as a catalyst, creating the possibility for the others to face up to what they have done. At times he seems in control of what they say – as Sheila says, 'Somehow he makes you' (p. 37). Think about how the way he uses the information makes him appear both an outsider and an all-knowing creature, mysterious and powerful.

EXAMINER'S TIP

Look at the stage directions. They give additional information to the actors, and in them you may find physical descriptions and suggestions about how a character is behaving and/or feeling.

GRADE BOOSTER

Think about other ways in which the Inspector appears to be different from our expectations of a police inspector.

GRADE BOOSTER

Give four or five words of your own which describe Mr Birling's **character**, behaviour or attitude.

 **DID YOU KNOW?**

In the early nineteenth century it was illegal in Britain for people to join a trade union. The penalty for doing so was to be transported to prison colonies in Australia.

Mr Birling

WHO IS MR BIRLING?

Mr Birling is a successful businessman, who has been active in local politics, has been Lord Mayor of Brumley and is the father of Eric and Sheila.

WHAT DOES MR BIRLING DO?

- Mr Birling hosts a dinner to celebrate Sheila's engagement to Gerald Croft.
- He declares that a man's responsibility is only to himself and his family.
- Two years ago he fired Eva Smith from his factory.
- He tries to intimidate the Inspector, but also tries to protect himself and his family.
- He becomes increasingly concerned about any possible scandal.
- He is the one who takes the final telephone call.

HOW IS MR BIRLING DESCRIBED AND WHAT DOES IT MEAN?

Quotation	Means?
'heavy-looking, rather portentous man' (p. 1)	Mr Birling's size helps to give him a threatening appearance.
'a hard-headed practical man of business' (p. 6)	He thinks of himself as a man who does well in business, and who doesn't let sentiment get in the way of whatever needs to be done to succeed.
'Yes, my dear, I know – I'm talking too much.' (p. 7)	He likes to air his views and is aware that he tends to monopolise the conversation, suggesting he has a high opinion of his own importance.
'I'm a public man – ' (p. 41)	He expects respect as he has been a member of the town council, Lord Mayor and a magistrate.

EXAMINER'S TIP: WRITING ABOUT MR BIRLING

When you are writing about Mr Birling, remember that he sees himself as an important man in Brumley and he is prepared to use his reputation and powerful friends to intimidate the Inspector. Notice how he makes his views clear in the early speeches in Act One, and these do not change. His cry that he would give the girl thousands of pounds if he could is because he is afraid of what the girl's death will do to him, his family and to his chances of getting a knighthood, not because he feels remorse over sacking her. Mr Birling represents what socialists, like J. B. Priestley, felt was wrong with society. He is a man with money, power and social position, but he has no sense of social justice.

Mrs Birling

WHO IS MRS BIRLING?

Mrs Birling is a prominent member of the Brumley Women's Charity Organization.

WHAT DOES MRS BIRLING DO?

Mrs Birling praises Gerald for his timing of the presentation of the ring.
She treats the Inspector as an inferior.
She is disgusted when she learns that Daisy Renton was Gerald's mistress.
She persuaded the Charity not to help the pregnant girl.
She blames the girl's death on the father of the child – who turns out to be her son.
She claims she was the only one not to 'give in' to the Inspector.

HOW IS MRS BIRLING DESCRIBED AND WHAT DOES IT MEAN?

Quotation	Means?
'a rather cold woman' and 'her husband's social superior' (p. 1)	Mrs Birling is not a friendly person and rarely shows any affection. She looks down on most people and expects the Inspector to treat her with respect.
'Please don't contradict me like that.' (p. 30)	She does not like, and doesn't expect, people to disagree with her. She is used to being listened to and having her opinions accepted as right.
'It's disgusting to me.' (p. 38)	Even though Gerald comes from a good family and meets with her approval as a future son-in-law, she cannot accept Gerald's affair.
'the most prominent member of the committee' (pp. 43–4)	She is the most powerful and respected member of the group which runs the Charity, and is able to influence the decisions it makes.

EXAMINER'S TIP: WRITING ABOUT MRS BIRLING

Show that, despite her charity work, Mrs Birling lacks understanding of how other people live, shown in her comments about 'a girl of that sort' (p. 47) and her unwillingness to believe the girl's reasons for refusing to take stolen money or to marry the young man responsible for her pregnancy. Her lack of understanding extends to her family as she has been unaware of Eric's heavy drinking. She remains untouched by the Inspector's questions, although she is shocked to learn of her son's involvement. Having condemned Gerald's 'disgusting affair' (p. 38), she forgets it once the threat of scandal has been removed.

★ GRADE BOOSTER

Look back at pages 1–7 of the play and pick out what Mrs Birling says and does to show how fussy she is about good manners and correct behaviour.

? DID YOU KNOW?

Helping in a charity was considered almost compulsory for wealthy women during the late nineteenth century and early twentieth century, but charities would help only people they thought of as the 'deserving poor', that is people who led honest lives and tried to help themselves.

Sheila Birling

WHO IS SHEILA BIRLING?

Sheila is the daughter of Mr and Mrs Birling and is engaged to Gerald Croft.

WHAT DOES SHEILA DO?

- Sheila shows genuine emotion when she hears that a young woman has died.
- She was responsible for making the girl lose her job in the dress shop.
- She realises the Inspector is not someone who can be lied to.
- After hearing about his affair, she breaks off her engagement to Gerald.
- She reveals that Eric drinks too much.
- She understands that the family's experience that night is meant to make them improve the way they treat others.

HOW IS SHEILA DESCRIBED AND WHAT DOES IT MEAN?

Quotation	Means?
'Oh – how horrible! Was it an accident?' (p. 17)	Sheila feels shock at the death of a young woman. She is naive to suggest that someone could drink a fatal amount of disinfectant 'by accident', but it shows she can't imagine someone not having a lot to live for.
'I wouldn't miss it for worlds' (p. 34)	Although bitter about Gerald's relationship with Daisy Renton, her curiosity needs to be satisfied and she is strong enough to hear the full story.
'I had her turned out of a job.' (p. 56)	She is prepared to accept responsibility for what she has done.
'it's you two who are being childish – trying not to face the facts'. (p. 59)	Sheila clearly believes that it doesn't matter whether the Inspector is a real police officer or not. Her parents are relieved that they might prevent a scandal, but she is concerned that they all harmed someone.

GRADE BOOSTER

Find examples of when Sheila is lively and excited; caring; frightened; gentle and sympathetic.

DID YOU KNOW?

The tradition of giving an engagement ring dates back to medieval Italy; the ring **symbolises** the promise of a never-ending future together.

EXAMINER'S TIP: WRITING ABOUT SHEILA

Note that Sheila changes more than any other **character**. At first she is playful and self-centred, enjoying the attention her engagement brings. When she hears of the girl's death she shows a sensitive side to her nature: she responds to the girl as a person, not as cheap labour, and criticises her father. When she realises her own jealousy and bad temper led to the girl losing her job, she is genuinely sorry. She grows stronger as the play goes on, and has the strength of character to respect Gerald's honesty, even though she feels they should end the engagement. She understands the Inspector's message, that there is a need for justice in society. These things all help to make her a more sympathetic character.

Eric Birling

WHO IS ERIC BIRLING?

[Eri]c is Sheila's brother. He is employed in his father's business,
[dri]nks more than is good for him and is the father of Daisy Renton's
[un]born child.

WHAT DOES ERIC DO?

Eric drinks too much at the family dinner.
He met the girl in the bar of the Palace Theatre and made her pregnant.
He stole money from his father's firm to give to the girl.
He accuses his mother of killing her own unborn grandchild.
He accepts his guilt, whether the Inspector is a real police officer or not.

Quotation	Means?
[J]ust keep quiet, Eric, [a]nd don't get excited' [p]. 13)	Mr Birling recognises that Eric has had too much to drink and might easily say something he shouldn't.
[T]hat's something this [p]ublic-school-and-['V]arsity life you've had [d]oesn't seem to teach [y]ou.' (p. 16)	Eric has been to an expensive school and then university, but Mr Birling feels he knows more of life than his son.
Besides, you're not the [t]ype – you don't get [d]runk – ' (p. 50)	We know that Eric does get drunk, and that the opposite of what his mother says is true.
Your trouble is – ['y]ou've been spoilt'. [(p]. 54)	Mr Birling thinks that by being the boss's son Eric has had too easy a life.

GRADE BOOSTER

Notice how J. B. Priestley manipulates his **characters**, having them going out of the room and coming back at moments which heighten the dramatic tension.

DID YOU KNOW?

We believe today that anyone with good exam results can go to university, but a hundred years ago relatively few young people had the chance to do this.

EXAMINER'S TIP: WRITING ABOUT ERIC

Think about Eric as a bit of a misfit. He is *'not quite at ease, half shy, half assertive'*
(p. 2). He is weak-willed and looks for an easy way out of troubles. He sees his father
as *'not the kind of father a chap could go to when he's in trouble'* (p. 54). Notice
how he doesn't share his father's *'hard-headed'* (p. 6) attitude to business and to his
employer. Notice also how the unpleasant side of his character is brought out when
he drinks. He insists on going home with the girl, but cannot remember what
happened that first time. He makes the girl pregnant and steals money from his
father's firm. When the girl suspects he has stolen the money she refuses to take any
more, and also refuses to marry him. Like Sheila, Eric believes that their experiences
at the hands of the Inspector should make them improve their behaviour.

GRADE BOOSTER

Gerald has much in common with Mr Birling. Look through the play and find instances when the two of them seem to think in the same way.

Gerald Croft

WHO IS GERALD CROFT?

Gerald is the son of a wealthy industrialist and business rival of Mr Birling, and he has just become engaged to Sheila Birling.

WHAT DOES GERALD DO?

- Gerald gives Sheila an engagement ring during the dinner party.
- He agrees with Mr Birling about the way a business should be run.
- He rescued Daisy Renton from the drunken Alderman Meggarty.
- He kept Daisy as his mistress for six months, then broke off their relationship.
- He finds out that a police sergeant has never heard of an Inspector Goole.
- He telephones the Infirmary and learns that no girl died that day.

HOW IS GERALD DESCRIBED AND WHAT DOES IT MEAN?

KEY CONNECTION

In *A Christmas Carol*, Charles Dickens gives the miser Scrooge the opportunity both to look back on his past life and forward to the future so that he is able to change his ways and so avoid the consequences of his meanness.

Quotation	Means?
'easy, well-bred young man-about-town' (p. 2)	Gerald gets on easily with people, is self-confident and assured, and looks as if he knows a lot about life.
'That was clever of you Gerald.' (p. 5)	He has a sense of what to do and when to do it, and he clearly has the approval of Mrs Birling.
'You're just the kind of son-in-law I always wanted.' (p. 4)	Mr Birling sees Gerald as being like himself – a determined man of business; he sees the engagement as bringing the two family businesses together.
'I'm rather more – upset – by this business than I probably appear to be – ' (p. 39)	Gerald has been hiding his feelings, like an English gentleman is expected to do. Deep down he is greatly saddened by the girl's death, and has a strong feeling of responsibility for what has happened.

EXAMINER'S TIP: WRITING ABOUT GERALD

Gerald is not a member of the family, but his engagement to Sheila, business interests and knowledge of the girl link him closely to them. He is a complex character. The others have acted out of greed, anger, jealousy, spite, lust or pride, but you could argue that Gerald was motivated by sympathy and then genuine attraction. His sensitive nature is shown in the way he produces the engagement ring, by his reaction to the death of the girl and by his gently asking Sheila if he can come back after she has returned the ring. Note that his admission of his relationship with Daisy impresses Sheila who admits 'I rather respect you more than I've ever done before' (p. 40). At the same time, he agrees that Mr Birling was right to sack Eva Smith, and worldly-wise enough to enquire about the Inspector and then to phone the Infirmary and lie about his interest in a possible suicide.

Eva Smith/Daisy Renton

WHO IS EVA SMITH/DAISY RENTON?

These are two names by which the girl who suffered at the hands of the Birling family and Gerald was known.

WHAT HAPPENS TO HER?

Mr Birling sacked her from his factory for leading a strike for better pay.

She was sacked from a dress shop after Sheila unjustly complained about her.

She became Gerald Croft's mistress.

She was made pregnant by Eric Birling.

She applied to a charity for help, but Mrs Birling refused that help.

She committed suicide by swallowing disinfectant.

HOW IS SHE DESCRIBED AND WHAT DOES IT MEAN?

Quotation	Means?
'a lively good-looking girl – country bred' and a 'good worker too' (p. 14)	Mr Birling had a good opinion of her. Being bred in the country made her naive, less worldly-wise than a city girl. As a good worker she was a potential 'leading operator'.
'She'd had a lot to say – far too much – so she had to go.' (p. 15)	She had spoken up for the other girls who were on strike and was showing leadership qualities against Mr Birling, and he didn't like that.
'She was very pretty and looked as if she could take care of herself.' (p. 24)	But Sheila judged the girl by her appearance, and she did not think about the difficulties the girl might face in getting another job.
'Now she had to try something else.' (p. 25)	The words sound innocent, but the 'something else' was meeting men in a place used by prostitutes.

EXAMINER'S TIP: WRITING ABOUT THE GIRL

The girl remains a mystery: she never appears on stage, we do not know her real name, but the play revolves around her. We do know she was pretty enough for Mr Birling to remember her, for Sheila to be jealous of her and to attract the attention of Gerald and Eric. What we learn about her contrasts sharply with what we see of the Birling family. We should also recognise that she worked hard, supported her fellow workers and was kind. Although she was reduced to earning her living by picking up men in the Palace Theatre bar, her honesty prevented her from considering marriage to Eric and protected him from his folly in stealing money. You could say that she stands for all the people we meet in our everyday lives, and J. B. Priestley uses her to make us think about our responsibility towards others.

GRADE BOOSTER

Think about the characters' deeper significance as well as what they do. To what extent do you think Eva Smith/ Daisy Renton is an 'every-woman' figure?

EXAMINER'S TIP

Remember that characters are revealed through what others say about them as well as what they themselves say and do.

Progress and revision check

REVISION ACTIVITY

❶ Select two ways in which the Inspector and Mr Birling are opposites of each other. (Write your answers below)

....

❷ Find two places where Mrs Birling's coldness of character can be clearly seen?

....

❸ What do Sheila's immediate reactions to learning of the girl's death tell us about her?

....

❹ What is there about Eric's first meeting with the girl that shows the worst side of his character?

....

❺ What do Gerald's actions in the final section of the play tell us about him?

....

REVISION ACTIVITY

On a piece of paper write down the answers to these questions:

● Why might we think Mrs Birling is a hypocrite?
Start: *Mrs Birling's behaviour can be seen to be hypocritical on several occasions ...*

● What do we see in Sheila's character which might make us take a critical view of her?
Start with: *Sheila has been very fortunate in her life ...* or *Our first impressions of Sheila are not particularly poor ones ...*

GRADE BOOSTER

Answer this longer question about characters in the play:

Q: How does J. B. Priestley create a feeling of sympathy for Eva Smith/Daisy Renton even though the audience never meet her? Think about ...

● The way different characters describe her.

● How each character treats her.

● The way the Inspector makes references to her.

For a C grade: Convey your ideas clearly and appropriately (you could use words from the question to guide your answer) and refer to details in the text.

For an A grade: Make sure you deal with each of the suggested bullets in depth and detail. Emphasise the ways the audience's picture of her is gradually built up and changes during the play, and offer your own interpretation of how she is seen by the end.

Key contexts

THE AUTHOR: J. B. PRIESTLEY

J. B. Priestley was born in Bradford, Yorkshire, in 1894. He left school at 16, worked for a firm of wool merchants then joined the army at the start of the First World War, serving in France where he was wounded and gassed. After the war he was awarded a place at Cambridge University. He took a degree in Literature, History and Politics, after which he became a journalist writing for publications such as *The Times Literary Supplement* and *The New Statesman*. His first play, *Dangerous Corner*, was written in 1932, and together with *I Have Been Here Before* and *Time and the Conways* make up his 'Time' plays which took inspiration from his fascination with theories about time, premonitions and the idea that some people could see into the future and so be able to recognise and change actions which might have terrible consequences. *An Inspector Calls*, written in 1945, has some elements of this idea. As a socialist, he was disappointed in the economic chaos, political unrest and social deprivation that followed the First World War and ruined the dream of a country fit 'for our heroes to live in'. This play may be seen as his plea, and his hope, for a fairer and more equal society once the Second World War was over. In all J. B. Priestley wrote over sixty books and more than forty plays.

SOCIAL POSITION

Social position, your place in society, was far more important in 1912 than it is today. Following the dramatic expansion of industry throughout the nineteenth century, many men in industries such as coal, iron and steel, pottery and textiles made considerable fortunes. Industrialists may have come from humble origins but their wealth allowed them to rise up the social ladder. Marriages between these newly rich families and aristocratic, but often impoverished, land-owning families helped to secure new social positions. Many of the industrialists were granted titles and this too helped to improve their social standing. It was important to maintain at least an outward appearance of respectability.

Arthur Birling has made his money through building up a successful manufacturing business. Mrs Birling's attitudes, her desire for strictly correct behaviour – even down to criticising her husband when he compliments the cook in front of a guest – and her general manner all suggest that she comes from a 'better' family background than Mr Birling. He has enhanced his status by getting on to the town council, becoming Lord Mayor and accepting the duties of a magistrate (an unpaid judge for minor offences). He is expecting his service to the community to be rewarded with a knighthood, which will raise him further up the social ladder. Gerald Croft's father is already a knight and the Crofts' firm is a larger one than Mr Birling's. A knighthood will make Sheila a more acceptable daughter-in-law for Lady Croft. Mr Birling's importance in the town and the influential friends he has made allow him and Mrs Birling to feel superior to the Inspector who they see as being only a public servant. His questioning brings out secrets that will cause a scandal and seriously damage the Birlings' social position.

KEY CONNECTION

As well as being a prolific writer, J. B. Priestley made radio broadcasts during the Second World War, founded his own production company and was the director of the Mask Theatre in London.

WORKERS AND BOSSES

At the time the play is set, the Labour Party, founded by James Keir Hardie in 1893, was only just beginning to make an impact on the political life of the country. The rights of workers, like Eva Smith, were not taken too seriously by many employers, but at the same time many working people had benefited from the generosity of industrialists who genuinely cared for the welfare of their workers. Workers, however, generally didn't have much job security, and being fired from a job meant you had no references to show you as being of good character, making it harder for you to find another job. There was no unemployment pay or benefits system to help you if you were out of work.

Mr Birling's firm employed 'several hundred young women' (p. 12) so his recognition of a girl he had sacked two years earlier suggests she stood out from the crowd. The women had no trade union to organise their strike, to negotiate their claim for higher wages or to give them financial support during the strike. Mr Birling saw his duty as being 'to keep labour costs down' and so saw nothing wrong in sacking the 'four or five ring-leaders' (p. 15). Gerald thinks Mr Birling is right to do that, but Eric and Sheila do not. Perhaps because of the qualities which led the foreman in Mr Birling's factory to think that Eva was worthy of promotion, and because of her pleasant manner and appearance, the girl was able to find a good job in the dress shop. Once Sheila had her sacked from that job she found it difficult to find other work, and we see how easy it would be for her to have to lead the sort of life which led her into the clutches of Alderman Meggarty, Gerald and Eric.

SETTING AND PLACE

The play is set in the fictional industrial town of Brumley. It is typical of the many towns where the factory owners, who provided much-needed employment, were able to run things pretty much as they liked. It is clearly a large town, having a Lord Mayor and its own police force and Chief Constable. The action of the play takes place in the Birlings' dining room, which is described in the stage directions as 'substantial and heavily comfortable, but not cosy' (p. 1), reflecting the family's outward comfort and inner tensions. J. B. Priestley wants the stage set to be realistic to convince the audience they are watching something real and normal – then he is able to create a greater effect when that normality is shattered.

GRADE BOOSTER

Create a single revision sheet for each of the key contexts and themes. You could set it out in the form of a diagram with essential quotations, key points and some of your own thoughts.

EXAMINER'S TIP: WRITING ABOUT SETTING AND PLACE

In the fictional town of Brumley we see opportunities for employment in factories, and the town has shops which cater to the rich. Notice that employment of any kind, however, is dependent on the whims of the factory bosses and the shops' rich customers. We see another aspect of the town in the Brumley Women's Charity Organization, which suggests there are women who are poor and in need of help. The girl's treatment shows that the poor cannot depend on getting that help. You can discuss the contrast between the power of the rich and way of life of the poor inhabitants of the town, illustrated by the comfortable home, elegant clothes and fine food we see in the Birling household, and the shabby living conditions and hunger endured by Eva Smith/Daisy Renton.

Key themes

AN EQUITABLE SOCIETY

In this play, J. B. Priestley presents us with a sincerely felt and powerfully expressed social message. We are shown the comfortable home and rich way of life of the Birling family. By contrast we have the accounts of the desperate attempts of workers to increase their poor wages and the drab and sordid life that the girl is forced to live as a result of the actions of such people as the Birlings.

The Inspector champions the cause of the poor, and tries to get the others to accept that all people share a common humanity and so are part of an interdependent community. This message seems to get through to Eric and Sheila, but their father dismisses the idea of a community, in which responsibility and guilt are shared, as the foolish mutterings of socialist cranks.

As the play progresses, the Inspector's point is put across more and more forcefully, and he becomes a spokesperson for the disadvantaged and a voice for the conscience which the Birlings and Gerald seem to lack. The Inspector points out what would happen if injustice and inequality were allowed to continue unchecked. His oratorical style might seem exaggerated and overpowering if J. B. Priestley had not gradually built up the mysterious and prophetic aspects of the Inspector's character.

KEY CONNECTION

Vincent Brome's biography *J. B. Priestley* (1988) is excellent for learning more about J. B. Priestley's life, especially his 'Time' plays.

EXAMINER'S TIP

Answer the question that has been set – not the one you wished had been set!

REVISION ACTIVITY

- Look at what the Inspector and Sheila say about the girl's situation and about 'cheap labour' (p. 19).

- Reread Sheila's account of the confrontation in the dress shop (pp. 23–4).

- Look again at Gerald's story of meeting the girl. Reread pages 35–7 and notice how different the girl's world is from Gerald's.

EXAMINER'S TIP: WRITING ABOUT AN EQUITABLE SOCIETY

It is clear that even today there are many things which we might see as being unfair. When looking at this play, however, it is important that we realise that the world Priestley was writing about wasn't just 'unfair'. It was a world in which most people had few rights, and they depended upon the goodwill of their employers far more than people do today. J. B. Priestley wants us to see that Eva Smith is completely at the mercy of the Birling family, and as she comes into contact with each of them her situation gets worse and worse. Notice how he takes Eva Smith on a downward journey; point out that when things seem to be going well for her something else will happen to spoil things for her.

GRADE BOOSTER

A feature of A-grade writing on literature is the ability to see more than one possibility of interpretation and to support a preference for one of them.

EXAMINER'S TIP

Short, or even single-word, quotations can be very effective if embedded into your own writing.

RESPONSIBILITY

Most of the **characters** have a narrow view of what it means to be responsible, but the Inspector provides us with a much broader one. Mr Birling feels his responsibility is to make a success of his business. This means making as much profit as possible, even if he is harsh in his dealings with those who work for him. As a family man he has a responsibility to provide for the material needs of his family, yet it is clear that Eric does not see him as the kind of father to whom he could turn when in trouble.

Mrs Birling accepts her responsibility as chair of the Women's Charity Organization, but sees only a responsibility to help those that she feels are deserving of help. She allows her personal feelings to prejudice her decisions. Sheila belatedly recognises that as a powerful customer she has an obligation not to let her personal feelings and ill-temper lead to misery for people who have no power, while Eric has little sense of responsibility at all. He drinks far more than is good for him and he forced the girl into a relationship which had disastrous consequences. He attempted to help her by stealing from his father.

Gerald showed some sense of responsibility when he rescued the girl from the unwelcome attentions of another man, fed her and found her somewhere to live. Yet he gave in to his own desire for personal pleasure and eventually abandoned the girl without knowing, or very much caring, what happened to her.

REVISION ACTIVITY

Go back and look up these examples of occasions when you can see some of the characters' attitudes towards responsibility:

- Mr Birling's speech on page 10 and Eric's echoing of that speech on page 58.

- Mrs Birling's views, towards the end of Act Two, on who is to blame for the girl's death.

- What we learn of Eric's behaviour towards the girl in Act Three.

LOVE

The play presents a variety of thoughts about love, the nature of love and different people's interpretation of love. Sheila and Gerald appear to be in love, and their engagement seems to bring them happiness as they contemplate their future together. After each of them has confessed to their shameful behaviour towards Eva Smith/Daisy Renton, Sheila realises that they do not really know each other well and that trust is an essential ingredient in a loving relationship. We are left wondering if their love will survive these events.

Mr Birling's remark about the engagement of his daughter bringing the two family firms into a closer working relationship gives us an indication of his attitude towards love and marriage. He sees marriage as a convenient way of progressing up the social and economic ladder. This makes us wonder whether love played any real part in his marriage to the socially superior Sybil Birling and whether her coldness to others, including her own children, does not have its roots in a loveless marriage.

oth Gerald and Eric have been involved with the girl, yet each of them denies that hey loved her – their relationships were prompted by physical attraction. The girl ook up with Eric out of necessity, but she does, however, seem to have felt a enuine love for Gerald. Gerald's ending of the affair may be seen as being callous in iew of her love for him.

he Inspector preaches a form of love, a sort of true 'charity' which is a deep care for ur fellow human beings. This is quite alien to Mrs Birling who is prepared to devote me to 'charity' while having no real care for others.

REVISION ACTIVITY

- Look at the way Gerald and Sheila talk at the time when he hands her the engagement ring (p. 5).

- Notice how Sheila, after hearing Gerald's story, realises that they don't really know each other (p. 40). Think about whether this suggests their love was true love or not.

- When Gerald is asked whether he loved Daisy Renton, he says 'It's hard to say. I didn't feel about her as she felt about me' (p. 38). Eric is more straightforward, saying 'I wasn't in love with her or anything – but I liked her – she was pretty and a good sport' (p. 52). What do we learn of the two men's attitudes?

TIME

B. Priestley wrote the play for an audience just coming out of the horrors of the econd World War, yet he set his play in 1912, two years before the start of the First World War: this brings us to a consideration of J. B. Priestley's use of time as an lement of his plays. At the end of the play we are left with a sense that the events re going to start all over again. We wonder whether things will be different and ow the characters will behave.

ne 'time' theory suggests that when we die we re-enter our life and live it all over gain, and only by doing things better can we escape that cycle and begin a new life n which we do not repeat our mistakes. Another theory states that you could be iven the gift of seeing forward in time as well as looking back. This would mean hat, just as you can look back and see what actions led to your present situation, you ould look forward and see the consequences of your actions. So, if you wished, you ould change those actions and avoid the consequences.

n Inspector Calls contains elements of these time theories. The Inspector, arriving efore the suicide is a reality, offers each character a chance to see the consequences, o change the future, to break the circle. Eric and Sheila seem prepared to face up to heir past actions and to improve themselves, but the others do not.

he reflections on the past, and the possibilities of the future, highlight the mportance of caring for others, of taking responsibility for our actions and of onsidering the consequences of them.

GRADE BOOSTER

A good answer will show that you can interpret and analyse points in the text, so avoid vague general statements.

EXAMINER'S TIP

It is always a good idea to collect a range of words to describe a character.

KEY CONNECTION

J. B. Priestley based his 'Time' plays on the ideas which P. D. Ouspensky expressed in his book *A New Model of the Universe* (1931) and on the theories of J. W. Dunne. Try finding out more about these writers.

EXAMINER'S TIP

When writing about a specific scene or extract always make connections with the play as a whole – this shows you have read the complete work.

REVISION ACTIVITY

- Consider what Mr Birling's speeches about the good times ahead, the prospects of lasting peace, the advance of technology and the newly launched 'unsinkable' *Titanic* meant to the audiences that first saw this play in 1946.

- Trace how the Inspector links each member of the family and Gerald to a specific time in the girl's life, and how the times fit so carefully together.

- Think of ways to explain the final telephone call.

EXAMINER'S TIP: WRITING ABOUT TIME

Think about the Inspector's knowledge of events, apparently before they happen, his steady revelation of the characters' pasts and their links to the dead girl over a two-year period. These things give him a mystical, unworldly quality.

Notice how the Inspector's departure leaves the characters free to decide their future, while at the end we are left to wonder how they will cope with reliving the close scrutiny of their dealings with others when the cycle of questions begins all over again.

It is worth commenting that by setting the play in 1912 and presenting it to a later audience, J. B. Priestley has covered an era which includes both world wars. The failure of the older characters to learn anything reflects the failure of generations to learn from the mistakes of the recent past. There is dramatic irony in that characters talk of hopes for peace and prosperity, but we know these will not happen. By 1945, J. B. Priestley was hoping that the second time around the world might learn from past mistakes and we might see such hopes realised if we, the audience, can accept the challenge to be caring and socially aware.

KEY CONNECTION

Television programmes such as *Doctor Who* and films such as *Back to the Future* use the idea of intervention by a superior being to bring about change in the lives of others. Films such as *Groundhog Day* use the notion of time being circular.

Progress and revision check

REVISION ACTIVITY

❶ How did Priestley earn his living after leaving Cambridge University? (Write your answers below)

....

❷ How has Arthur Birling made his money?

....

❸ Who was responsible for founding the Labour Party in 1893?

....

❹ Which famous ship sank on 14 April 1912?

....

❺ In which town is the play set?

....

REVISION ACTIVITY

On a piece of paper write down the answers to these questions:

● How might Mr Birling be seen as typical of men who in 1912 had confidence in the future?
Start: *Mr Birling shows his confidence in the future during Act One when he says …*

● What evidence can you find to suggest that Brumley is a large and prosperous town?
Start: *We know that Brumley is a large and prosperous town because …*

GRADE BOOSTER

Answer this longer practice question about the setting of the play:

Q: What is the effect of setting the whole play within Mr Birling's house? Think about …

● How the house and its contents are described and what this tells us.

● How it contrasts or links to other settings in the play.

For a C grade: Explain clearly what effect the setting has, supporting your main points with relevant quotations and examples.

For an A grade: Explore each of the suggested points in depth and detail, and make a personal response to the symbolic importance of the house and other settings mentioned.

Language

Here are some useful terms to know when studying *An Inspector Calls*, how they appear in the text and what they mean.

Literary Term	Means?	Example
Imagery	Creating a word picture; common forms are metaphors and similes	Sheila warns her mother not to try 'to build up a kind of wall' (p. 30)
Irony	When someone says or does something and the audience understand more than is apparent to the speaker or character	The girl's request for help is turned down by the woman who would be the grandmother of her child
Symbolism	Use of an object or person to represent something else, possibly an idea or quality	The girl stands for all oppressed women, while the Inspector (the police officer) represents those who seek to uncover the truth and bring wrongdoers to justice
Euphemism	A word or phrase which is less blunt, rude or frightening than the actual subject	Gerald uses the euphemism 'women of the town' (p. 34) as a polite way of saying prostitutes

EXAMINER'S TIP

A play has a number of high points – look for where a series of actions leads to a dramatic climax.

LANGUAGE AND CHARACTER

The language used by each **character** helps us form a clearer picture of them. J. B. Priestley gives his characters realistic language, though it may sound a little strange to our ears because the realistic language of 1912 is not the everyday realistic language of our times.

The Inspector, we are told, speaks *'carefully, weightily'* (p. 11) and what he says consists largely of questions and instructions. This helps him to control, direct and develop the plot. His words are often matter of fact, which is what we expect from a police officer, but his tone is commanding and even threatening. In his final sermon-like speech he uses the language of a prophet or missionary.

t times his short, sometimes single-word sentences are replaced by long sentences which produce a rhythm to give what he says extra emphasis and makes what he says ery logical, e.g. 'Because what happened to her then may have determined what appened to her afterwards, and what happened to her afterwards may have driven er to suicide'. These words are followed by the terse comment 'A chain of events' (p. 4), and we can see that the logical sequence links up just like the links of the chain.

EXAMINER'S TIP: WRITING ABOUT MR BIRLING'S LANGUAGE

You can contrast the speech of the Inspector with that of Mr Birling who, we are told, is *rather provincial in his speech* (p. 1) and frequently speaks in a bullying and forceful manner. His language lacks the sophistication which Gerald finds quite natural, and he gives the impression of someone who wants to sound like a solid, middle-class Edwardian gentleman but never quite convinces us that he is.

ANGUAGE AND EDWARDIAN MANNERS

eople were rather more aware of good manners in 1912, and we can see several stances when what characters say can be interpreted as well-mannered or not. ght at the start Mr Birling quite innocently compliments his wife and the cook on e 'very nice' meal. His wife tells him off because they have a guest present, but erald, the guest, has the social skill to gloss over Mr Birling's mistake (pp. 2–3).

erald, then, seems to be someone whose language is always polite and correct, but B. Priestley allows him to be less polite when he is describing Alderman Meggarty's ehaviour with the girl. By doing this J. B. Priestley allows us to guess the depth of eling that Gerald had for her.

ang expressions, such as 'squiffy' (p. 3), 'Don't be an ass' (p. 3) and 'chump' (p. 5), e used more by the younger characters, though Mr Birling is guilty of occasional oses such as 'fiddlesticks'. When Eric and Gerald use **euphemisms** in referring to ings of a sexual nature, especially in the presence of the ladies, they are trying to nsure that the ladies are not shocked or discomforted. Earlier in the play, the spector declares she 'became Daisy Renton, with other ideas' (p. 33) for exactly the me reason. Eric's 'She wasn't the usual sort' (p. 51) begs the question as to what the sual sort' is, whereas when Mrs Birling refers to 'a girl of that sort' (p. 47) we know actly what she means.

r Birling angrily asks Eric 'So you had to go to bed with her?' (p. 52), avoiding being y more explicit but also questioning him bluntly. So even in a 'man to man' scussion it would seem there were boundaries, even though Eric has been rather ore blunt with his description of 'fat old tarts' (p. 52).

EXAMINER'S TIP

Always allow yourself time to check your work. If you are working at home, read your essay out aloud; if in an exam or a classroom, read over your words silently and slowly.

EXAMINER'S TIP: WRITING ABOUT THE LANGUAGE OF LOVE AND AFFECTION

Look out for the language of love in the play. Sheila and Gerald show considerable affection in the early part of the play. They joke with and tease each other. When the engagement ring is presented, Sheila speaks in a way which is full of emotion, her sentences broken up, disjointed and incomplete. Noice that when Gerald realises that the girl is dead, he speaks in the same broken, disjointed way. This may suggest his genuine affection for Daisy Renton. Sheila's language to Gerald is different when she feels her love has been betrayed. Then she is more in control, and we see the fury of a woman scorned.

The conversations between Mr Birling and his wife lack any of the emotion we see in Sheila and Gerald. You might like to question whether this suggests an emotionless, cold marriage or the easy and undemonstrative manner of a couple who have been married for a long time.

LANGUAGE AND DRAMATIC IRONY

Much of the play's success depends upon the dramatic irony which J. B. Priestley creates. We see this in Arthur Birling's flamboyant expression of his faith in technology and scientific advances leading to a prosperous peace stretching far into the future. Just like the audiences who saw the play when it was first written, we know he is mistaken, and so we guess that other views are equally wrong.

When Sheila has worked out that Eric might well be the father of Daisy Renton's child, we see the irony in that Mrs Birling has not realised and is unwittingly demanding that an example be made of her own son. The contrast between Sheila's increasingly excitable language, Mrs Birling's high-handed and moralistic language and the Inspector's calm, controlled and understated comments increases our awareness of the dramatic irony being played out for us.

Perhaps there is a different sort of irony in the fact that the Inspector has been talking as much to us, the audience, as to the characters. We have to ask ourselves whether we are in a position to judge what has happened when we are probably as guilty of acting irresponsibly and unkindly as anyone on the stage. This irony strengthens our feeling that J. B. Priestley's type of socialism is not so much about politics but about caring and even, perhaps, about love.

Structure

THE PLOT

This play follows the tradition of what is known as a **well-made play**. It has a plot in which the action flows smoothly and all the parts fit together precisely, rather like parts of a jigsaw puzzle. As a result, the **characters** and the audience move from a state of ignorance to a state of knowledge. J. B. Priestley wanted his play to have a uniformity of manner and tone with one situation rapidly moving on to the next. The **unities** of time and place are achieved by the events all taking place in the dining room and the action running continuously through all three Acts.

THE INSPECTOR'S ROLE IN THE STRUCTURE

The action is taken forward by the Inspector's questioning of each character in turn. Their reasons for entering or leaving are always plausible and allow a new aspect of the plot to be introduced or something mentioned earlier to be developed. The play is built up in a series of episodes when each character has either a leading or supporting role, even in their absence. Gerald's decision to go for a walk, for example, means that he can alter the course of events after the Inspector's departure, while Eric's similar absence allows his involvement with Eva Smith/Daisy Renton to be explored in a way that it could not be if he were present. Each new revelation, prompted by the Inspector's careful use of the photograph or diary, adds to the overall picture of two crucial years in the girl's life. As the pattern develops, we in the audience are able to predict what will happen next.

THE CHANGING MOOD

J. B. Priestley brings about quite subtle changes of mood. The play begins in a mood of high celebration but, after the Inspector's entrance, the other characters have little reason for self-congratulation and the mood becomes more sombre, even threatening. By the time the Inspector delivers his final speech the mood has become one that promises danger for the future. The relief that is felt when the Inspector is seemingly shown up as a hoaxer and no evidence of a suicide can be found is shattered by the final dramatic telephone call. J. B. Priestley uses **stage directions** to suggest how the lighting effects can reflect the mood. He orders *'pink and intimate'* (p. 1) lights for the party, changing to *'brighter and harder'* (p. 1) when the Inspector's investigation begins.

TWISTS IN THE PLAY

Although the action and the time span of the play are realistic, J. B. Priestley throws in two twists at the end. First, we have the problem of who the Inspector really is: a trickster determined to make fools of the family or an avenging spirit come to make them see the evil of their ways? The second twist is the time-release mechanism when the telephone call interrupts and takes the family back to relive the events. It is this which allows the possibility that the Inspector is a real police officer who has stepped out of real time and will return. If they fail to learn from their experiences and are *'ready to go on in the same old way'* (p. 71) the Inspector's threat of *'fire and blood and anguish'* (p. 56) will become their reality.

EXAMINER'S TIP

Some examination questions have prompts to help you. Don't ignore them but use them as a starting point for planning your answer.

EXAMINER'S TIP: WRITING ABOUT THE PLAY'S STRUCTURE

Remember that the key points regarding the structure of *An Inspector Calls* are the way the action progresses in real time and the building of the chain of events. As each **character** is about to come under the scrutiny of the Inspector, there is a build-up of tension and then a gradual settling down to the revelations that inevitably come. J. B. Priestley uses the Inspector to keep everything neatly ordered and he signals that this is how things will be early on when the Inspector makes it clear that his way of working is 'One person and one line of enquiry at a time' (p. 12).

DIALOGUE

It is worth considering the way that a playwright structures the characters' dialogue. Look at the section leading up to the Inspector's final speech. Notice how J. B. Priestley has rapid exchanges involving the Inspector and the Birling family, and how the dialogue, with its repetitions, short sentences and varied mood swings, seems so realistic.

The contributions by each of the family involve accusations and admissions of guilt and regret, and all of this gives the Inspector more on which to build his final speech. Notice also how Priestley uses his **stage directions** to ensure that the actors deliver their lines in a way which gradually adds to the tension of the situation, which leads to the farewell speech with its tone of a church sermon.

Rhetoric is the art of speaking or writing effectively in order to persuade an audience. It is used in the dialogue of this play. A frequently used rhetorical device is the linking of things together in threes. The Inspector's accusation that Eric had used the girl 'as if she was an animal, a thing, not a person' is made more effective by those three elements which follow Eric's triple use of 'killed' when he is accusing his mother (p. 55). In his final speech, the Inspector uses 'millions and millions and millions' to further stress the vast numbers of helpless girls like Eva Smith. He goes on to provide three ways of showing how people are linked: 'We don't live alone. We are members of one body. We are responsible for each other.' He then warns that if men don't learn that lesson then it will be taught 'in fire and blood and anguish' (p. 56). You will recognise this is a powerful metaphor, as is the Inspector's earlier use of paying a 'heavy price' and 'a heavier price still' (p. 56).

Progress and revision check

REVISION ACTIVITY

❶ What does the first section of the play (pp. 1–7) establish?
(Write your answers below)

....

❷ What is Mrs Birling's reaction to Sheila's use of slang?

....

❸ How far back in time does Mr Birling's link with the girl take us?

....

❹ Give an example of a euphemism.

....

❺ Why does Priestley have Gerald leave the house before the end of Act Two?

....

REVISION ACTIVITY

On a piece of paper write down the answers to these questions:

● How does Sheila's language reveal her changing emotions?
Start: *At the start of the play when Sheila is happy her language is simple and relaxed …*

● In what way could we say that the plot comes full circle (returning to where it started)?
Start: *The play begins with the Birling family in a mood of celebration …*

GRADE BOOSTER

Answer this longer question about the structure of the play:

Q: How does J. B. Priestley ensure that the Inspector's 'chain of events' is convincing? Think about …

● The order in which the Inspector questions each character.

● The use of repetition.

For a C grade: Convey your ideas clearly and appropriately (you could use the words from the question to guide your answer) and refer to details from the text (use specific examples).

For an A grade: Make sure you comment on the varied ways the play is structured, on the development of the plot and on how each character takes the plot forward. If possible come up with your own original or alternative ideas.

PART SIX: GRADE BOOSTER

Understanding the question

Questions in exams or controlled conditions often need **'decoding'**. Decoding the question helps to ensure that your answer will be relevant and refers to what you have been asked.

 ### UNDERSTAND EXAM LANGUAGE

Get used to exam and essay style language by looking at specimen questions and the words they use. For example:

Exam speak!	Means?	Example
'convey ideas'	'get a point across to the audience': usually you will have to say how this is done	Sheila's statement that the girls 'aren't cheap labour – they're *people*' (Act One, p. 19) *conveys* the idea that workers deserve to be treated with humanity.
'methods, techniques, ways'	the 'things' the playwright does: making characters enter or leave at crucial moments, ending a scene on a cliff-hanger, or having a character say something which has more than one meaning	The playwright might create tension in the words of characters before someone's entrance – as Priestley does with Mrs Birling's condemnation of the unborn child's father just before Eric enters at the end of Act Two.
'purpose'	the reason 'why' a writer does something	Priestley introduces the 'rough sort of diary' (Act Two, p. 39) to provide the Inspector with knowledge not available to the others. This makes him more powerful than the person he is questioning.

 ### 'BREAK DOWN' THE QUESTION

Pick out the **key words** or phrases. For example:

Question: How does Priestley use the **changes in Sheila's character** to **convey** a belief that **a just society** in the future depends upon the behaviour of **the younger generation**?

● The focus is on **Priestley's views** about **society**, so you will need to talk about what those views are, what Priestley felt was wrong with society and what he hoped for in the future.
● You are asked to respond by looking at how **Sheila's character changes**.

What does this tell you?
● **Focus** on the changes to Sheila's character – when and how these happen and what Priestley wants us to think about these changes.

 ### KNOW YOUR LITERARY LANGUAGE!

When studying texts you will come across words such as dialogue, dramatic irony and imagery. Some of these words could come up in the question you are asked. Make sure you know what they mean before you use them!

Planning your answer

is vital that you **plan** your response to the controlled assessment task or exam uestion carefully, and that you follow your plan, to gain the higher grades.

 ## DO THE RESEARCH!

Vhen revising for the exam, or planning your response to the controlled assessment ask, collect **evidence** (for example, quotations) that will support what you have to ay. For example, if preparing to answer a question on how J. B. Priestley has xplored the theme of social justice you might list ideas as follows:

Key point	Evidence/quotation	Act, Scene etc.
Mr Birling has a selfish view of society	'a man has to mind his own business and look after himself and his own'	Act One, p. 10

 ## PLAN FOR PARAGRAPHS

se paragraphs to plan your answer. For example:

- The first paragraph should **introduce** the **argument** you wish to make.

- The paragraphs that follow will **develop** this argument. Include **details, examples** and other **points of view**. Each paragraph is likely to treat one point at a time.

- **Sum up** your argument in the last paragraph.

or example, for the following task:

uestion: How does J. B. Priestley present the character of Sheila? Comment on the language devices and techniques used.

Simple plan:
- Paragraph 1: *Introduction*
- Paragraph 2: *First point*, e.g. Initially, J. B. Priestley presents Sheila as lively, excited, pleased with life. Her language is conversational, she uses slang, she jokes.
- Paragraph 3: *Second point*, e.g. On hearing of the girl's death she shows herself sensitive to the girl's situation. J. B. Priestley shows her feelings of guilt through her frank confession of how she treated the girl in the shop.
- Paragraph 4: *Third point*, e.g. Sheila's bitterness at Gerald's behaviour shows how she has been hurt, but her generous nature is shown by her fair-minded assessment of Gerald. Her ability to think of others is also shown by her attempts to protect Eric from her mother's condemnation of the 'young man'.
- Paragraph 5: *Fourth point*, e.g. J. B. Priestley demonstrates how the Inspector's visit has had a great effect on Sheila. Her earnest pleas to the others are made in language which echoes that of the Inspector, indicating that she has taken his views on board.
- Paragraph 6: *Conclusion*

How to use quotations

One of the secrets of success in writing essays is to use quotations **effectively**. There are five basic principles:

❶ Put quotation marks, e.g. ' ', around the quotation.

❷ Write the quotation exactly as it appears in the original.

❸ Do not use a quotation that repeats what you have just written.

❹ Use the quotation so that it fits into your sentence, or if it is longer, indent it as a separate paragraph.

❺ Only quote what is most useful.

 **USE QUOTATIONS TO DEVELOP YOUR ARGUMENT**

Quotations should be used to develop the line of thought in your essays. Your comment should not duplicate what is in your quotation. For example:

GRADE D/E	GRADE C
(simply repeats the idea)	**(makes a point and supports it with a relevant quotation)**
Gerald Croft is embarrassed to admit that he met Daisy Renton in the spring in the stalls bar of the Palace music hall: 'I met her first, sometime in March last year, in the stalls bar at the Palace' (Act Two, p. 34).	Gerald Croft is embarrassed, but admits that he first met Daisy Renton 'sometime in March last year, in the stalls bar of the Palace'.

However, the most sophisticated way of using the writer's words is to embed them into your sentence, and further develop the point:

GRADE A

(makes a point, embeds quote and develops the idea)
Gerald Croft is embarrassed to admit he met Daisy Renton 'sometime in March last year' when he had gone into 'the stalls bar of the Palace', a local theatre with a bad reputation.

When you use quotations in this way, you are demonstrating the ability to use text as evidence to support your ideas – not simply including words from the original to prove you have read it.

★ GRADE BOOSTER

Where appropriate refer to the language technique used by the writer and the effect it creates. For example, if you say, 'this metaphor shows how ...', or 'the effect of this metaphor is to emphasise to the reader ...' this will get you much higher marks.

EXAMINER'S TIP

Try using a quotation to begin your response. You can use it as a launch-pad for your ideas, or as an idea you are going to argue against.

Sitting the examination

xamination papers are carefully designed to give you the opportunity to do your
est. Follow these handy hints for exam success:

 ## BEFORE YOU START

- Make sure you **know the texts** you are writing about so that you are properly prepared and equipped.

- You need to be **comfortable** and **free from distractions**. Inform the invigilator if anything is off-putting, e.g. a shaky desk.

- **Read** and follow the instructions, or rubric, on the front of the examination paper. You should know by now what you need to do but **check** to reassure yourself.

- Before beginning your answer have a **skim** through the **whole paper** to make sure you don't miss anything **important**.

- Observe the **time allocation** – and follow it carefully. If the paper recommends 45 minutes for a question make sure this is how long you spend.

GRADE BOOSTER

Don't be afraid to develop your own views. Try to show different interpretations of the play or of events within it, but make sure you can always support your theories with evidence.

 ## WRITING YOUR RESPONSES

A typical 45 minute essay is probably between 550 and 800 words long.

Ideally, spend a minimum of 5 minutes planning your answer before you begin.

Use the question to structure your response. Here is an example:

Question: Do you see the ending of the play as negative or positive? What methods does the writer use to lead you to this view?

- The introduction could briefly describe **the ending** of the play;

- the second part could explain what could be seen as **positive**;

- the third part could be an exploration of the **negative** aspects;

- the conclusion would **sum up your own viewpoint**.

For each part allocate paragraphs to cover the points you wish to make (see **Planning your answer**).

Keep your writing clear and easy to read, using paragraphs and link words to show the structure of your answer.

Spend a couple of minutes afterwards quickly checking for obvious errors.

 ## 'KEY WORDS' ARE THE KEY!

Keep on mentioning the **key words** from the question in your answer. This will keep
you on track and remind the examiner that you are answering the question set.

Sitting the controlled assessment

It may be the case that you are responding to *An Inspector Calls* in a controlled assessment situation. Follow these useful tips for success:

 ## WHAT YOU ARE REQUIRED TO DO

Make sure you are clear about:

- The **specific text** and **task** you are preparing (is it just *An Inspector Calls*, or more than one text?)

- How **long** you have during the assessment period (i.e. 3–4 hours?)

- How **much** you are expected or allowed to write (i.e. 2,000 words?)

- **What** you are **allowed to take** into the Controlled Assessment, and what you can use (or not, as the case may be!). You may be able to take in brief notes but not draft answers, so check with your teacher.

GRADE BOOSTER

Produce a list of at least three key moments, three key quotations and three opinions of your own on each character.

 ## HOW YOU CAN PREPARE

Once you know your task, topic and text/s you can:

- Make **notes** and **prepare** the **points**, **evidence**, **quotations**, etc. you are likely to use.

- Practise or draft **model answers**.

- Use these **York Notes** to hone your **skills**, e.g. use of quotations, how to plan an answer and focus on what makes a **top grade**.

 ## DURING THE CONTROLLED ASSESSMENT

Remember:

- **Stick** to the topic and task you have been given.

- The allocated **time** is for **writing**, so make the most of it. It is double the time you might have in an exam, so you will be writing almost **twice as much** (or more).

- **If** you are **allowed** access to a **dictionary or thesaurus** make use of them; if not, don't go near them!

- At the end of the controlled assessment follow your **teacher's instructions**. For example, make sure you have written your **name** clearly on all the pages you hand in.

Improve your grade

is useful to know the type of responses examiners are looking for when they award
fferent grades. The following broad guidance should help you to improve your
ade when responding to the task you are set!

GRADE C

What you need to show	What this means
ustained response to task nd text	You write enough! You don't run out of ideas after two paragraphs.
ffective use of details to upport your explanations	You generally support what you say with evidence, e.g. Sheila opposes her father's views when she defends the workers as people, not 'cheap labour' (Act One, p. 19).
xplanation of the writer's use of language, structure, orm, etc., and the effect on readers	You must write about the playwright's use of these things. So, you might comment on the Inspector's careful, measured use of language compared to the excitable way that Eric speaks, or you might point out the way Priestley manages to make each set of questions neatly link with what has gone before and what is to follow.
Appropriate comment on characters, plot, themes, deas and settings	What you say is relevant. If the task asks you to comment on how the Inspector builds his 'chain of events' (Act One, p. 14), you don't need to describe his appearance but you should concentrate on the way he links all the incidents in the girl's life.

GRADE A

What you need to show in addition to the above	What this means
Insightful, exploratory response to the text	You look beyond the obvious. You might question the idea of of the Inspector being more than an ordinary police officer, perhaps exploring his almost superhuman knowledge.
Close analysis and use of detail	If you are looking at the writer's use of language, you comment on each word in a sentence, drawing out its distinctive effect on the reader, e.g. the use of the word 'offence' as used by Mrs Birling and the Inspector in Act Two, p. 31.
Convincing and imaginative interpretation	Your viewpoint is likely to convince the examiner. You show you have *engaged* with the text, and come up with your own ideas.

Annotated sample answers

This section provides you with extracts from two **model answers**, one at **C grade** and one at **A grade**, to give you an idea of what is required to achieve different levels.

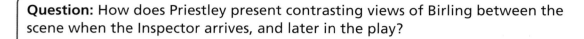

Question: How does Priestley present contrasting views of Birling between the scene when the Inspector arrives, and later in the play?

CANDIDATE 1

Sound opening point

Priestley shows in the opening scene that Mr Birling is not worried by the Inspector's visit because Birling offers him a drink. He thinks the Inspector has come for a warrant, something a magistrate like Mr Birling could provide. We see from what Birling says about himself that he is self-important. He makes sure the Inspector knows that he was an alderman, a 'Lord Mayor two years ago'. He is putting himself above the policeman who he thinks is there to ask a favour of him. He is surprised to learn the Inspector has come to ask questions about a girl's suicide, and even when he knows that he sacked her from his factory two years before, he isn't able to see that her death has anything to do with him. This suggests he only sees his workers as there to make him money. He is prepared to drop hints about playing golf with the Chief Constable, and to warn the Inspector, and this shows he will use his important friends to protect himself and give him an unfair advantage. Adjectives such as 'impatiently' and 'restlessly' about how he speaks show that he is used to getting his own way.

Quite thoughtful comment, but not supported or developed

Later on, he shows he is angry when Eric sides with the girls who went on strike and shows that he doesn't think Eric has learnt much from his 'public-school-and-Varsity' education. Sheila also takes the girls' side and Birling is not so hard with her and tries to protect her from the worst details about the girl's death, so Priestley shows he has a gentler side to him. We didn't see this so much at the start when he was showing off.

Relevant quotation here

Priestley also reveals more about Birling through what the Inspector says. He has his own way of working, and questions each character in turn. As he does this each is seen to have some responsibility for doing harm to the girl, even Birling. This evidence makes us see that Birling's idea that 'a man has to mind his own business and only look after himself and his own' is not right if 'his own' means just his family. The Inspector shows that it should mean those he has responsibility for, and that includes the people he employs. The Inspector is making a case for the sort of protection which workers today can expect to have. Priestley uses the Inspector to put forward his own views, and the Inspector's final speech sums up, like a sermon, all that was wrong with what Birling was doing.

Suggests the relevance of the play to modern audiences

Evidence? Add scene and further quotation.

Contrasting views of Inspector but this is an essay on Birling

Evidence of personal response

Overall comment: Candidate shows fair understanding of the text and makes some perceptive comments. Quotations are mostly appropriate but the effect not always commented on. The response tends to retell the story a little but a clear impression of Birling's character is developed, although there is too much on the Inspector. Perhaps greater attention to supporting evidence would have helped and more on the language used.

GRADE C

CANDIDATE 2

(This is the first part of a student's response, dealing with the first scene.)

Strong and engaging opening

The opening extract shows Mr Birling in an increasingly bad light. In keeping with the mood of celebration at the dinner, Priestley shows that Birling's initial greeting of the Inspector is warm enough as he is 'still on the Bench' and as a magistrate sometimes has to sign warrants for the police. His assumption about the warrant allows Birling to act like someone enjoying the power of being in a superior position, placing the Inspector in the role of someone seeking a favour, and this is exemplified by the adjectives to describe his way of speaking and behaving – i. e 'impatiently', 'restlessly'. However, he is surprised to learn the true reason for the Inspector's visit, and the way Priestley changes the direction of the plot and the change of mood, reverses their positions placing the Inspector in control, something clearly resented by Mr Birling.

Good use of language technique to show character

Effective focus on structure and mood

Both his actions and what he says further support the picture we have seen at the start. Having recognised Eva Smith's photograph, his explanation of how he sacked her not only backs up his earlier assertion that he is a 'hard-headed man of business' but also reveals how a man who prides himself on his status in the community can still be ruthless in pursuit of 'lower costs and higher profits' even if this unfairly penalises his workers. Priestley also conveys his cunning, shown by his realisation that the strike could not last since after the holidays 'they'd all be broke' and this adds to the impression of a heartless and ruthless man.

Insightful comment on characterisation

Other characters also help build a picture of Birling in the opening section. Eric's defence of the workers brings about a vicious verbal attack from Birling which pours scorn on Eric's lack of business experience and reveals his bitter feeling towards the 'public-school-and-Varsity' education. Priestley suggests he resents the advantages enjoyed by his son's generation and this helps the audience understand why later Eric says that Mr Birling is 'not the kind of father a chap could go to when he's in trouble'.

Well developed argument

At this point, Priestley has provided a picture of a self-important man who places his faith in technology and industry, who believes that he can enjoy the rewards granted by the community while declaring that community spirit is 'nonsense' and that a man has to 'mind his own business and look after himself and his own'. Yet Eric, at this start of the Inspector's 'chain of events', has already challenged his father's views, and later Sheila will do the same by recognising a shared humanity with the workers.

Strong sense of dramatic construction

Overall comment: This is an interesting study of Mr Birling which displays the ability to understand his motives and behaviour. Quotations from the text are used skilfully to develop and secure the argument, and demonstrate the candidate's ability to form personal and original responses. The close reference to language and its effects, and comment on what the author does to build the picture of Birling, show this to be a sophisticated response to the first part of the task.

GRADE A

Further questions

EXAM-STYLE QUESTIONS

1. Which of the characters is most affected by the events of the evening?
Write about:
- What the Inspector's visit reveals about the different characters
- How each is affected
- Why you feel any one character is affected more than others

2. How does the play show up the contrast between the philosophies of Mr Birling and Inspector Goole?
Write about:
- What Mr Birling thinks is important in life
- What the Inspector believes is important in life
- What message the playwright intends us to take away with us

3. What aspects of British society does the play criticise?
Write about:
- Things that J. B. Priestley, through the Inspector, sees as bad
- Things various characters think of as important
- Your views on which things you might agree with

4. Describe the way J. B. Priestley develops Sheila's character during the course of the play.
Write about:
- What Sheila is like at the beginning of the play
- What things affect her during the play
- What sort of character Sheila seems to be at the end of the play

5. Examine the evidence to decide whether Eva Smith and Daisy Renton are indeed one and the same person.
Write about:
- How each character knew Eva or Daisy
- What the Inspector told them about the girl
- How the Inspector got his evidence

CONTROLLED ASSESSMENT-STYLE QUESTIONS

1. Explore the ways in which the witches in *Macbeth* may be seen as a similar dramatic device to Eva Smith/Daisy Renton in *An Inspector Calls*.

2. Explore how the historical setting of *An Inspector Calls* and that of any of Shakespeare's plays might affect a modern audience's response to and appreciation of the themes and ideas within the two plays.

3. Explore how the theme of social status is used to add dramatic effect in *An Inspector Calls* and in Shakespeare's play *Twelfth Night*.

4. Explore the importance of family ties in *Romeo and Juliet* and *An Inspector Calls*.

5. Explore the ways in which the ending of any Shakespeare play which you have read and the ending of *An Inspector Calls* are, or are not, dramatically satisfying.

Literary terms

Literary term	Explanation
characters	either a person in a play or novel, etc. or his or her personality
coup de théâtre	a sudden and spectacular turn of events in the plot of a play
dialogue	speech and conversation between characters
didactic	writing or speech intended to teach or instruct
dramatic irony	occurs when the development of the plot allows the audience to possess more information about what is happening than some of the characters have themselves
euphemism	unpleasant, embarrassing or frightening facts or words can be concealed behind a 'euphemism' – a word or phrase less blunt or offensive
imagery	creating a word picture; common forms are metaphors and similes
irony	consists of saying one thing while you mean another, often through understatement, concealment or indirect statement
monologue	lengthy speech by one person
oratory	the dignified, formal style used by someone making a speech in a public place
polemic	a piece of writing expressing an argument about important social issues such as religion or politics
sarcasm	an extreme form of irony, usually intended to be hurtful
stage directions	advice printed in the text of a play giving instructions or information about the movements, gestures and appearance of the actors, or on the special effects required at a particular moment in the action
symbolism	use of an object or person to represent something else, possibly an idea or quality
theme	a central idea examined by an author
the unities	in Classical Greek drama, plays conformed to the unities of action and time – one complete action happening in a single day or night. The unity of place was added later
well-made play	a play that exhibits a neatness of plot and smooth-functioning exactness of action, with all its parts fitting together precisely. *An Inspector Calls* works through an interlocking series of unexpected discourses, leading to a final revelation that is almost a trick ending
whodunnit	a novel, play etc. concerned with crime, usually a murder

Checkpoint answers

CHECKPOINT 1
- Mr Birling is a self-important man.
- He has a strong belief in his own position of power.
- He wants to be accepted into society and is proud of his humble start in life.
- He has a narrow view of the world.
- He prefers to believe what suits his purpose.

CHECKPOINT 2
- The Inspector uses the expression 'a chain of events' (Act One, p. 14) quite early on.
- The method of questioning each member of the family in turn adds to this sense of there being a chain.
- The deliberate mention of the time of each event links what one character has done to what the next one questioned has done.
- There are aspects of the girl's description, manner or behaviour that are common to more than one character's memory of her.

CHECKPOINT 3
- Eva Smith died in the Infirmary after swallowing disinfectant.
- She had left a letter, a photograph and a diary.
- She had used more than one name.
- She had been employed in Mr Birling's factory and was sacked in September 1910 for asking for higher wages.
- Both her parents were dead.
- She had been out of work for two months, had no savings and was becoming desperate.
- She had got a job at Milwards but had been sacked in January 1911 after a customer complained about her.
- She had changed her name to Daisy Renton and had decided to try another kind of life.

CHECKPOINT 4
- The Inspector decides who will be questioned and when.
- He decides who will or will not see the photograph.
- He makes Mr Birling recognise the implications of others possibly being involved in the 'chain of events' (Act One, p. 14).
- He contradicts Birling and overrules his wish that Sheila should leave the room.
- His method of questioning draws confessions from Mr Birling and Sheila.
- He makes it clear he will not leave until he gets to 'know all that happened' (Act One, p. 25).
- His way of dropping in the name of Daisy Renton catches out Gerald.

CHECKPOINT 5
Birling:
- Is reluctant to discuss his business.
- Refuses to see that he has done wrong.
- Is unmoved by the girl's death.
- Has little concern for what might have happened to the girl after he sacked her.
- Is casual about the idea that the girl may have had to 'Go on the streets' (Act One, p. 16).
- Is concerned only about his business and his profits.

Gerald:
- Tells the story fully, after a brief attempt at denying knowledge of the girl.
- Is clearly distressed when the fact of the girl's death sinks in.
- Does not blame the girl for what happened between them.
- Stresses the girl's good points.
- Shows care and compassion in his tone.
- Recognises how important he became to the girl.
- Admits she behaved better than he did.

CHECKPOINT 6
- Sheila admits she disliked Gerald after his reactions to her own confession and her realisation that he had had a relationship with the girl.
- She says she now respects him more and acknowledges he has been honest.
- She accepts his motives were originally good ones and she recognises that by revealing their secrets each now sees the other in a new light.

CHECKPOINT 7
- The father is described as being young.
- He is 'silly and wild' (Act Two, p. 46) and we have seen Eric being silly at the dinner party.
- He drinks too much and is a 'drunken young idler' (Act Two, p. 48).
- He comes from a different social class from the girl's.

CHECKPOINT 8
- Mrs Birling talks down to Sheila and the Inspector and looks down on those, like the girl, who are in trouble.
- She calls the Inspector 'impertinent' (Act Two, p. 30).
- She speaks 'haughtily' (Act Two, p. 30), 'grandly' (p. 31) and 'sharply' (p. 32).
- She claims to have done nothing wrong and tries to pass the blame on to anyone other than herself.
- She says the girl has only herself to blame, concentrating on blame instead of helping someone in trouble.
- She says, of the father of the unborn child, 'If the girl's death is due to anybody, then it's due to him' (Act Two, p. 48)
- She admits to being prejudiced.

CHECKPOINT 9
- Sheila feels it makes no difference. She recognises that they have all done wrong. She feels that he was their inspector (that is, he inspected their behaviour), whether he was a police officer or not.
- Eric supports Sheila. He sees the need for them all to change their behaviour.
- Mr Birling sees that if the Inspector is not a real police officer there is less chance of a scandal over their dealings with the girl. He foresees no scandal relating to the money stolen from the firm's office. He persuades himself it has all been 'an elaborate sell' (Act Three, p. 70), that is a trick.
- Mrs Birling supports her husband. She feels that if the Inspector was an imposter then she has been right to behave as she has.
- Gerald is excited by the prospect that there has not been any official investigation. He appears to believe that the Inspector being a fake puts things right.

CHECKPOINT 10
- Sheila and Eric accept responsibility.
- They do not feel that anything has happened to relieve their guilt.
- They realise the seriousness of their actions and have taken the Inspector's message to heart.
- They have an understanding that the need to change their behaviour in the future.
- J. B. Priestley uses these two as symbols of the hope for a better future that lies in a younger generation.